Adirondack Treasure

ADIRONDACK
TREASURE
• THE BONAPARTE LEGACY •

A NOVEL BY
Matthew J. Glavin

Pyramid Publishing Inc.
Utica, New York

Copyright © 2012 by Matthew J. Glavin.
Second Printing: November 2012

ISBN: E-book 978-1-4653-7758-6
ISBN: Print Book 978-1-886166-33-2

This is a work of fiction. With the exception of the historical figures, names, characters,
places and incidents either are the product of the author's imagination or are used ficti-
tiously, and any resemblance to any actual persons, living or dead, events, or locales is
entirely coincidental.

This book was printed in the United States of America.

Cover Image: "Big Tupper" original watercolor © 2012 by Jeanne Reynolds.
Used with Permission.

Pyramid Publishing Inc.
PO Box 8339
Utica, New York 13505
www.pyramidpublishingservices.com

Dedicated To

My Mother
Helen Hartnett Glavin

My Father
James Edward Glavin

ACKNOWLEDGEMENTS

MY WIFE Stacy, and my sons, Christopher and Sean, provided constant encouragement throughout the process of writing of this book. My dad, Jim Glavin, made sure the historical facts about the Adirondacks and Joseph Bonaparte were accurate. He knows more about the Adirondacks than any man I know.

My brothers and sisters, Kathy, Timothy, David, Martin and Maureen, were "forced" to read chapters as they were written. Their honest criticism was important and valuable.

My nephew, Brendan Glavin, generously provided his unique insight. His comments made the book better. The character in the book, Brendan, is almost as sharp a man as the real Brendan he is based on.

This book would not have been written without the enormous help of New York State Trooper, Mike Dolan. Mike helped me understand the workings of the New York State Police. His generosity with his time and vast knowledge is greatly appreciated. Without question, Mike Dolan is the second best trooper in New York State. The best, of course, is the protagonist in *Adirondack Treasure*, Jerry Doolin. The only difference between Mike Dolan and Jerry Doolin is that Jerry is a fictional character. The similarity between Mike and Jerry's last names is intentional, as are the similarities between Mike and Jerry.

The incredible Bibi Wein edited the book. I'm not completely sure Bibi knew what she was getting into working with a first time author. She has insight and patience that are beyond words. At times, I thought she was reading my mind. Her remarkable talent made this book readable. Thank you, Bibi.

Nathaniel Bartlett Sylvester wrote a book in 1877 titled, *Historical Sketches of Northern New York and the Adirondack Wilderness.* It was Sylvester's chapter on Lake Bonaparte and King Joseph Bonaparte that provided the seed of an idea and prompted me to research the subject further.

Ron Arnold has been Executive Vice President of the Center for the Defense of Free Enterprise since 1984. Ron has gained wide recognition as an effective fighter for individual liberties, property rights and limited government. I met Ron in the early 1990's at a meeting in Seattle, Washington where he gave me a copy of his book, *Ecology Wars.* The book had an enormous impact on me and provided the inspiration (and even some of the dialogue) for the developer verses environmentalist storyline in this book. Thank you, Ron.

A special thanks to Karen and Jean Soltau, former owners of Stone Manor Diner in Cranberry Lake, New York. Thank you also to Suzie Thaller and Jeff Rabideau, the new owners of the diner. Every morning at coffee, they all had to listen to my ramblings about *Adirondack Treasure.* Thank you for your patience. See you there for breakfast.

Frank Spear, PhD, Chairman of the Geology Department at Rensselaer Polytechnic Institute in Troy, New York, helped me with the shift in magnetic north. Christopher Westbrook, director of The Ranger School in Wanakena, New York, also helped. Director Westbrook not only responded to my e-mail, he took the time to meet with me at The Ranger School. Thank you both.

The original watercolor of Mt. Morris and the Big Tupper ski area used for the cover was painted by Jeanne Reynolds. Jeanne has been painting

Adirondack scenes for more than sixty years. Be sure to visit her "End of the Pier" studio on Rt. 3 in Cranberry Lake when you're visiting. Thank you, Jeanne.

Thank you to Rita and Bob Kahute, who drove me the four hours from Cranberry Lake to the hospital in Rochester, New York, in the middle of writing this book.

And, to my sister-in-law Kim Glavin, who provided comfort during my hospital stay in Rochester, thank you. Your kindness will always be remembered.

PROLOGUE

FROM THE late-fifteenth century through the mid-eighteenth century, Spanish Conquistadors and explorers settled in the New World. Spanish kings laid claim to lands from South America through Mexico and what is now the Southern United States. In addition to vast landholdings, these monarchs were recipients of untold amounts of gold, silver and jewels brought back by faithful warriors.

Even today, lost Spanish galleons are regularly discovered with hundreds of millions of dollars in treasure. These lost ships represent only a small fraction of those returning from the New World. Most made an uneventful journey back to Spain to fill the coffers of the Spanish Royal Treasury.

§

After the success of the American Revolution, middle class French citizens grew anxious and demanded their voices be heard. On July 14, 1789, the Bastille was stormed by French artisans. Aristocratic property was seized and looted throughout France. In 1793, Louis XVI was beheaded, followed months later by the beheading of his Queen, Marie Antoinette.

Political strife continued throughout France until November 9, 1799 when a young general exploited political divisions by participating in a military coup and appointing himself "First Consul." In 1804, Napoleon declared himself Emperor of France. Thus began the Napoleonic era. A succession of military victories extended Napoleon's control to most of Europe.

Following victory in Naples in 1806, Napoleon gave his older brother, Joseph, military command of Naples. Shortly afterward, Joseph was made King of Naples and Sicily. Two years later, with the successful French invasion of Spain and the defeat of the Bourbon King, Ferdinand VII, Napoleon "promoted" Joseph to King of Spain.

King Joseph Bonaparte's reign was tenuous at best. With several military defeats to his credit, Joseph received additional troops from his Emperor brother, which enabled him to retake most of the country. Although Joseph tried to endear himself to the Spanish people by bringing an end to the Spanish Inquisition, his foreign birth guaranteed he would never gain the popularity he so desired.

After his defeat at the Battle of Vitoria in 1813, King Joseph fled Spain with the Royal Treasury and returned to France. He was replaced by Ferdinand VII, of the old Bourbon dynasty. The Napoleonic adventure would come to a close in 1815 with the battle of Waterloo.

Joseph, however, was still on the loose and seeking a place of refuge.

§

During the American Revolution, James Donatien Le Ray, Comte de Chaumont, supported the cause of liberty with such zeal that he committed most of his large fortune to the fledgling nation. In fact, it was at the grandiose French estate of the Count de Chaumont at Passy, that Benjamin Franklin resided while he served as the American representative to the French Court.

Shortly after the war his son, James D. Le Ray de Chaumont, traveled to America to settle his father's accounts. While here, he purchased several hundred thousand acres of land in northern New York State.

Traveling in France in 1815, de Chaumont heard that his good friend, ex-King Joseph Bonaparte, had arrived in the city of Blois. Paying respects to his dear friend, de Chaumont was invited by Joseph to dine. During their meal, Joseph suddenly remarked "I remember you spoke to me of your great possessions in America. If you still have them, I should like very much to purchase some in exchange for part of the silver in those wagons outside. Take four or five hundred thousand francs and give me the equivalent in land."

"I can't do that," replied Le Ray. "It is impossible to make a bargain when only one party knows what it's about."

"Oh," said the fugitive king, "I know you well enough, I rely more on your word than my own judgment."

In December 1818, a deed for a 150,000 acre tract of land, with a lovely lake in the foothills of the Adirondack Mountains in upstate New York was executed to Pierre S. Duponceau, confidential agent for the former King of Spain.

By the end of that year, the fugitive King had moved to an American estate called Point Breeze, located near the confluence of Crosswicks Creek and the Delaware River in Bordentown, New Jersey. He expanded his new home adding secret rooms, basement vaults and a secret tunnel to the river.

Point Breeze was destroyed by fire in January 1820, and newspaper accounts reported that the royal crown of jewels and the royal robes survived the blaze, having been "hidden in a secret room" and rescued through "an underground stone archway, seventy feet long, that ran from the house to the high rocky banks of Crosswicks Creek." These accounts go on to say that "the contents of the ex-king's vaults were rolled down this tunnel and saved that night."

Eight years later, under the assumed name of Count de Survilliers, King Joseph Bonaparte built a spectacular log lodge on the shores of the upstate New York lake he'd purchased from his good friend Le Ray years earlier.

Locals tell of the "Count" arriving with an "extensive entourage in carriages, each drawn by six horses."

§

Today, what was once the king's land encompasses the Town of Diana in Lewis County, New York. At Joseph's request, the town was named for Diana, the Roman goddess of hunting. The lake is now called Lake Bonaparte. To the east of the lake is the Bonaparte Cave State Forest where, it is said, the fugitive king eluded hired Bourbon assassins by hiding in the rocky ledges and small caves. These assassins had been charged not only to kill Joseph, but to recover the Spanish Crown and the rest of the lost Spanish Royal Treasury. They failed on both counts.

The cache was never found and rumors of its location have been part of local lore ever since King Joseph returned to France, in 1838. To this day treasure hunters continue to search the caves of the State Forest and the bottom of Lake Bonaparte.

While in America, King Joseph fathered a daughter, Caroline Charlotte who married Col. Zebulon Benton. The Benton family, originally from Ogdensburg, New York, settled in Jefferson County. Princess Caroline Bonaparte Benton and her husband Zebulon are buried in the graveyard of the old Presbyterian Church in Oxbow, New York.

ONE

NOBODY HEARD the body fall from the boat. There was no splash, and the lake was deep at this point. Instead of floating, the figure disappeared quickly in the deep water. The concrete blocks were doing their job. With the approaching storm the lake was unusually dark at 4:05 a.m. It was the third week in March and ice out was early so the water was still quite cold. The person in the boat knew the cold water meant the body would stay under longer because of slower bacteria growth and less bloating. But the body would come up eventually. They always do.

Despite the early hour, Jerry Doolin was sitting on his porch overlooking Cranberry Lake enjoying his morning coffee and the solitude. Weather permitting, this morning ritual helped him clear his mind of the cobwebs of sleep. He was wearing a heavy parka and the cool air was refreshing. He had been watching the boat's movements for about ten minutes.

In all his years living on the lake he had never seen a fisherman out this early in the season, or this early in the morning for that matter. Fishing season didn't open for another week. He thought he saw something being lifted over the side of the boat but, illuminated only by the boats running lights, at what he guessed was three hundred yards away, he couldn't be sure.

His friends always kidded him about seeing things where there was nothing. That was his way. Maybe it was because of his twenty-two years as a New York State Trooper or maybe because he was naturally curious. "It was probably just a bait bucket," he thought.

His shift started at five a.m. and his habit was to be at the barracks thirty minutes early with plenty of time to change into his uniform. Jerry refilled his coffee mug. During the forty-five-minute drive to the barracks in Tupper Lake he could not shake the feeling that something was wrong with what he had seen earlier. Who was in that boat? It was just an aluminum fishing boat and there were hundreds like it on the lake. This boat, however, would have a few new dents in the bow because there were still large chunks of ice just under the water's surface. There was no way that boat could have gotten to the middle of the bay without hitting a number of them.

Cranberry Lake is at the western edge of the Adirondack Park in northeastern New York State. This is a quiet and remote part of the Adirondacks. The lake itself was really the result of the dam built in the late 1800s by lumber interests. There are varying estimates about the size of the lake. Some say fifty-five miles of shoreline, others say 165 miles. The fifty-five milers are actually right, but 165 miles looks better in guidebooks for the tourists.

On the north end of the lake is the hamlet of Cranberry Lake. Jerry Doolin lives on Columbian Road on the northwest corner of the lake, only about a mile from the dam.

Over two thousand people lived here during the summer and Jerry didn't know most of them. Most owned summer camps that dotted the shoreline. Only about two hundred people lived here year round, and they were a bit resentful of the seasonal crowd, although the money they brought to the community was critical to their economic survival. This tension between "townies" and "summer people" occurs in hundreds of tiny communities throughout the Adirondacks.

When he was about half way to Tupper Lake, the rain began to fall.

Still, Doolin wasn't looking forward to another day of paperwork. He missed being in the field. That's where the fun was. That's where you met the people. Ever since his promotion to sergeant six years ago he felt he didn't belong.

The announcer from the North Country Public Radio station was droning on about another Adirondack Park Agency hearing next week for a massive new Tupper Lake development. Jerry pressed the button for the jazz station.

He hadn't been in the barracks ten minutes when his cell phone rang. Looking at the display he smiled to himself and answered, "Morning Joey."

"It's Joseph," the caller said. Joseph Benton hated being called anything other than Joseph so his best friend loved to kid him. Jerry knew he was the only person in the world who could get away with it.

"What's up buddy? It's early, even for you."

"Just checking to see if we're still on for Friday?"

"No problem, I'll be there early. You make the coffee, I'll bring the donuts"

"Why am I not surprised the cop offers to bring the donuts?"

"I'm a trooper, not a cop."

"And I'm Joseph, not Joey."

"Touché, see you Friday, Joe Boy."

"Thanks. See you then, copper."

Jerry had no intention of eating any donuts but he knew Joseph loved them.

Jerry was a fit five foot eight inches tall and looked younger than his forty-eight years. His shaved head was his most distinguishing feature, one he took a great deal of kidding about. His friend Joseph Benton was at the top of the list when it came to the "bald" jokes.

Benton lived in a large log cottage on Lone Pine Road on the shores of Cranberry Lake with his twelve-year-old cat, Bailey. He had built the cottage almost twenty years ago.

The home was directly across the north end of the lake from his buddy Jerry Doolin. A mixture of Adirondack-style furniture, antique French tapestries and junkyard-quality art filled the rooms. Dirty dishes in the sink, a half-empty bottle of Absolut vodka on the kitchen counter, piles of magazines on the floor next to every piece of furniture, and maybe the messiest desk in the Adirondacks contributed to the lived-in look.

On the desk, buried under piles of papers and folders was the computer keyboard. Rising out of the mess were two oversized screens used to follow his investments. Perched on the credenza behind the desk was his open laptop. Every computer screen had the words "Forever Wild" floating like dead fish. The "Forever Wild" screen saver was a recent addition to impress the lady he was now seeing.

Press any button and "Forever Wild" would be replaced with the Coat of Arms of Joseph Bonaparte, former King of Spain.

His friends joked that there was an area of the house for every subject. Piled on the bookshelves to the right of the desk were two years of *The Economist*. On the nearby chair was a stack of recent *Wall Street Journals*. This was the financial corner. Facing the flat screen TV was a leather recliner with a stack of Adirondack magazines on a side table and fifty or sixty *National Geographic* magazines in piles on the floor. The "naturalist" chair. Half of the upholstered sofa was covered with old *Time*, *Newsweek*, *U.S. News & World Report* and *The National Review* magazines. This was the current events area.

The table in the dining area was more like a library table covered with forty or so United States Geologic Survey topographic maps of the Adirondacks. Joseph had always loved the outdoors, particularly hiking the nearby wilderness areas. He was a solitary man and usually would take these hikes by himself. Next to the maps was an oversized Mickey Mouse coffee mug filled with pens, pencils and colored markers. Resting on the maps were a compass, a protractor and several rulers. The maps were dog-eared and covered with odd colored marks and lines. Well used, to say the least. Joseph knew this part of the Adirondacks as well as any man in the area.

Like most mornings lately, Joseph was nursing a hangover. After his brief conversation with Jerry, he logged onto his computer to check the futures before the markets opened.

Joseph Benton was a fifty-one-year-old out-of-work bum. At least that's how he thought of himself these days. For Benton there had been good years, a few very good years in fact, but after an ugly divorce, and a few big investments gone sour in a very bad economy, he had hit hard times. It was much worse than when the dot-com bubble burst in the late nineties. Most of the time he had that sick feeling in his stomach, the feeling you get when something goes horribly wrong. Although he had a Masters degree in economics, he'd never actually had a real job. He spent his entire adult life on his computer playing the stock market. A day-trader if you will, although he preferred to tell friends he was a financial analyst who worked from home. Over the past thirty years he had steadily squandered the sizeable inheritance he'd received when his mother died.

After placing a few buy and sell orders it was time to move on to the family research project. This was a project he had been involved with for the past thirty years. Because of his current financial situation, the "family project" had taken on much greater importance. In fact, it had become an obsession.

Joseph Benton was the only living descendent of Joseph Bonaparte, former King of Spain. His home in Cranberry Lake was forty miles east of the ancestral home at Lake Bonaparte. Little material evidence remained of his family history, save a few ancient tapestries, a single gold coin commemorating his famous ancestor's coronation to the Spanish throne, and a two-hundred-year-old family bible.

It was what he believed to be the least valuable of the items, the bible, that interested Joseph most. Inside the front cover was a handwritten note. While Joseph had a working knowledge of French, the note didn't appear to make sense. Inside the back cover was a drawing of a rather unusual disk with random numbers and symbols around the outer edge. In the center of the disk was a drawing of squiggly lines with a diagonal line to a pyramid with an "X" in the middle.

The tapestries, coin and bible had come to Benton after his mother's death. Along with the mysterious bible and a large cash estate, he'd also inherited the family legend—the story of buried treasure he'd heard about since childhood. Over the years, Joseph had spent hours simply staring at the message, the strange drawing and its numbers, wondering what they all meant.

He'd always wondered, "Could the legend be true?"

Nine a.m. and the markets open in just half an hour, Joseph thought. Also, today is the day he planned to begin cleaning his storage area. "It's time to get rid of most this crap," he muttered to himself. The divorce had been ugly. "The fewer reminders I have of that bitch, the better."

Joseph was under pressure to get this done because it was Tuesday and Jerry was coming over on Friday with a pickup to haul the bad memories to the transfer station, the twenty-first century incarnation of the dump. It was much more fun, he thought, when you could go to a real dump and watch bears clawing through the garbage.

He returned to his computers as the markets opened, but there would be nothing on the screen about his single biggest investment, the one that worried him most—over two million dollars invested in a real estate consortium out of New York City. The consortium had a few smaller properties, but the vast majority of their funds were committed to the largest single development ever proposed inside the Adirondack Park. In the planning stages for almost ten years, it was being held up by the state-run Adirondack Park Agency and the liberal non-profit group, Adirondack Environmental Watch. The APA was created by the New York State Legislature to oversee development of the three million acres of private land within the six-million-acre park. Unable to get further financing before APA approval, the developers were running out of money. If approval didn't come soon, the project was doomed.

While Joseph's two-million-dollar investment could make or break him, his interest in the project involved much more. So much, that the one stipulation he'd made with his investment was that his name would never publicly be associated with the project.

TWO

WITH LESS than a week before the court review of the shovel ruling in *Adirondack Environmental Watch, et al v. Adirondack Mountain & Lake Resort*, Maureen McCalister was looking forward to meeting her new staff. She'd arrived in Tupper Lake the night before and was staying in a lovely cottage provided by the Resort's developers.

McCalister knew this would be a difficult assignment. If the court hearing went well, her husband and two teenage boys would soon be joining her for the duration of her stint as project manager. If it went badly, it would be her job to shut down the project and leave no evidence they were ever there.

The developers had hired McCalister thinking a female project manager would soften their image. Maybe too little too late, she thought. The project had been in the planning stages for almost ten years and the developers had taken a beating in the press. The APA had demanded one environmental study after another, and Adirondack Environmental Watch, a radical environmentalist non-profit, had sued to stop the project.

After the first five years of legal wrangling, Judge Robert Kelly had issued an injunction stating that "not one shovel of dirt shall be turned on the property," until the case was resolved. The injunction soon became known as the "shovel ruling." Finally, after five more years of motions and counter-motions, thousands of pages of environmental studies, and hundreds of hours of expert testimony and cross examination, next week's hearing would decide everything.

The developer's attorneys assured her they had even odds of a successful outcome. She's not a lawyer, but she had her doubts.

Maureen McCalister was a large woman. Not fat, just tall and big boned. Her auburn hair, sweet personality and soft eyes didn't quite seem to go with the body.

This morning, Maureen planned to introduce herself to the small Resort staff. Confidently, she headed down the hall to the elegantly appointed conference room where the staff was already assembled waiting to meet their new boss. The all male team had been together for most of the past ten years. She knew she had a delicate balancing act, representing the new softer image of the corporation while appearing to be a tough manager.

Eight thirty a.m. Showtime, Maureen thought.

The employees had left the chair at the head of the table empty for her. On the wall was a large colorful rendering of the master plan for the Resort.

"Good morning, everyone," Maureen introduced herself and then asked each person at the table to give a short introduction of themselves. As the last person finished, she took a deep breath before continuing. "Gentlemen, I have been hired to soften the public persona of the Adirondack Mountain & Lake Resort. Make no mistake, I will do that. But do not, I repeat, do not take that to mean we are going to soften our stance on this project. As developers, we have a moral, ethical and financial obligation to protect ourselves from environmentalist attacks.

"I'm sure you know we owe that to the people of Tupper Lake. We owe that to our investors as well.

"What you may not know is that I spent fifteen years in the "belly of the beast." I was once a radical environmentalist. I led the largest environmental group in northern California. Before I resigned, I learned we can oppose radical environmentalism without opposing the environment."

"Let me share something with you that most people just don't understand. It is values, beliefs, attitudes and emotions that rule in social and political discourse, NOT facts and information. When businesses like ours are attacked by environmental organizations, high level managers often seem to lose their minds. They say such ridiculous things like, 'We won't stand for this.' 'Let's tell our side of the story.' Gentlemen, the reality is, this battle between developers and environmentalists amounts to all out war, and we will never win merely by telling our side of the story. Beginning today, we fight fire with fire.

"In the past, business tried to co-opt the environmental movement. They donated millions of dollars to environmental groups like the Sierra Club and Environmental Watch. Adirondack Mountain & Lake Resort even gave a hundred thousand dollars to Adirondack Environmental Watch trying to buy their support for this project. As I told our corporate owners in New York: What idiots! They gave rope to the hangman.

"A new day has arrived gentlemen.

"I have heard that some of you refer to the executive director of Adirondack Environmental Watch as Ms. Bitch. Gentleman, you ain't seen a bitch until you've seen me at work.

"Now, are there any questions?"

Craig Werner, a surveyor, spoke up. "Maureen, you said you were involved in the environmental movement but you left. I'm just curious . . . why did you leave?"

"That's a fair question. I know how they think. I left because of the blatant hypocrisy of the movement."

Maureen looked around the room and there were no other questions. "I look forward to working with each of you. Now, we have a lot to do, let's get to work."

"That went well," she thought. Shane Baxter, a New York City "hot-shot" lawyer walked back to her office with her. Baxter was a classic "city lawyer" quite out of place in the rustic and easy-going Adirondacks with his pinstriped, custom-made silk suits.

"That was a no-nonsense introduction," Baxter said.

"No point in beating around the bush, don't you agree?" McCalister had a habit of asking for agreement from whoever she was speaking to."

"You bet. But I have to ask, where's that sweet personality I heard so much about from upper management?"

"I save her for the press and the public. She won't be here for a few days. I've got some real work to do first. Like I said, you ain't seen a real bitch yet."

"That's scary. By the way, I understand you're planning on lunch with Ms. Bitch this afternoon. Do you really think that's wise?"

"I've got to get to know her sometime. Actually, I'm looking forward to it. I've heard so much about her I want to meet her for myself. A great military strategist once said if you know yourself and know your enemy, you will not fear the results of battle. Baxter, tell me, have you ever read Sun Tzu's, *Art of War*?"

"I've heard of it, but never read it."

"You should. In fact, I'd like you to read it before the hearing next Monday. It will give you an entirely new perspective on this war. I'll get you a copy this afternoon. When I get back from lunch I want to get together with you for an update on the hearing."

"Sure, see you then . . . enjoy your lunch."

In her office, Maureen pulled a file from her briefcase. She still had many friends in the environmental movement and had asked one good friend to put together a dossier on Ms. Bitch, Alicia LaCroix, executive director of Adirondack Environmental Watch. Maureen had read the file several times but wanted a final look before meeting her in person.

LaCroix had been executive director of Adirondack Environmental Watch for six years. Originally from Portland Oregon, she had a background as a lawyer for some of the most radical organizations in the environmental movement. She'd headed one from which several members had been arrested and convicted for criminal trespassing, reckless endangerment, first-degree assault and a whole host of other charges, all for tree spiking. She was lucky. She too had been arrested, but she'd been acquitted. Prosecutors couldn't prove to a jury, beyond a reasonable doubt, that she had ordered the attacks.

Tree spiking is the practice of hammering ceramic spikes into old growth trees marked for logging. Ceramic is used instead of metal because once the loggers figured out what the environmentalists were doing, they'd simply check the trees with metal detectors before they were cut. Ceramic spikes are hard to spot and they did little or no harm to the tree. However, when the tree is cut and the spiked logs go through the band saw at the mill, the blade would hit the spike and shatter, sending pieces of razor sharp steel in all directions. In one Oregon mill several workers were severely injured. One mill worker even lost an arm. Of course, the purpose of spiking was to discourage logging.

Ms. LaCroix apparently believes that private landowners have no right to cut trees on their own property. The whole concept of private property rights and the Fifth Amendment to the Constitution is alien to these people, Maureen thought. "These people are terrorists, not environmentalists," she mumbled to herself. "I wonder if Ms. Bitch lives in a house made of wood?"

Ms. Bitch is what the Resort employees called her, but Maureen knew from the dossier that LaCroix was very well respected in the environmental and legal communities. She had an impressive resume and even successfully argued a case before the United States Supreme Court. The Washington office of Environmental Watch had been recruiting her to take the position of national general counsel.

The dossier made it clear LaCroix was not a person to be taken lightly, and her organization was vehemently opposed to development of any kind at Big Tupper Ski Area. Moreover, recent polling showed that Adirondack Environmental Watch had a very high approval rating with the public.

One item in the dossier caught Maureen's interest yet again. For the past six months, Alicia LaCroix had been seeing a financial analyst named Joseph Benton. The relationship had been steadily escalating but LaCroix wanted to slow it down. She'd told friends she genuinely liked this guy. But, with the Resort case coming to a head, she didn't want the distraction from work. Regardless of how the judge ruled next week, there would be appeals to deal with. And, Cranberry Lake is more than an hour's drive from Saranac Lake where LaCroix lived.

"Maybe we can use this," McCalister thought. She had no idea Joseph Benton was a major investor in the Adirondack Mountain and Lake Resort. In fact, McCalister had never seen a list of investors. She had only met senior management of the development company. Individual investors were none of her concern.

Maureen looked at her watch. Eleven a.m. and lunch was scheduled at the Crowne Plaza Hotel in Lake Placid, more than an hour away.

THREE

JOSEPH BENTON had spent the past three hours cleaning the storage area in the basement of his home. Most of the items set aside for trash were things that reminded him of his ex-wife, Sharon. Joseph knew the reason for the divorce was what Sharon called his silly obsession. They'd split up two years ago, just when he was making huge progress in his search. For a while, Joseph thought they might reconcile. It wasn't until recently that he'd finally come to terms with the inevitable. The marriage was over, the bitterness was not. The drinking helped wash away the memories.

Joseph never thought of the treasure as an obsession. He knew in his heart the legend was true. After all, it had been passed down through five generations of the Bonaparte and Benton families. He had heard the story hundreds of times since he was a small child. He thought about it constantly. Wagons of gold, silver, jewels, even the royal crown, all taken when King Joseph Bonaparte fled Spain. There was the purchase of land in the Adirondack foothills. The fire in the house in New Jersey and the recovery of the treasure from that fire. The arrival of horse-drawn wagons at the magnificent log home on Lake Bonaparte must have been a spectacle. Then, there was the hiding of the treasure after word arrived that a team had been dispatched by King Ferdinand VII of Spain to recover the treasure and kill King Joseph. The former King himself had hidden from these assassins in the forest caves just east of the lake.

Locals were well aware of the legend. Many a treasure hunter had spent their vacation searching the hills by the ancestral home on Lake Bonaparte. Those hills are now known as the Bonaparte Cave State Forest, a 1435 acre state forest with hiking trails and terrific fishing. A few had gone diving, believing the treasure was at the bottom of the lake, but most, it seemed, were convinced the treasure was somewhere in the hills. Joseph himself had spent many a summer hiking this rugged area. Now, though, after thirty years of searching, he knew better.

Locals didn't know about the family bible with the note and the medallion allegedly telling where the fortune was hidden. The note inside the front cover was written in French and signed by King Joseph himself . . .

> *Ce bon livre est la carte pour votre liberté,*
> *le Seigneur Dieu vous montre le chemin,*
> *le médaillon est votre guide,*
> *Dumas est votre clé.*

Joseph had the note translated . . .

> *This good book is the map to your freedom,*
> *The Lord God shows you the way,*
> *The medallion is your guide,*
> *Dumas is your key.*

For years, he had studied the note in both French and English, but it made little sense. The first two lines were straightforward. The third line, "the medallion is your guide," clearly referred to the medallion drawn inside the bible's back cover.

The medallion was about four inches round. Along the circumference was a series of numbers, separated by comas, periods, ampersands, apostrophes, and question marks. In the center was what appeared to be a simple map with its squiggly lines and a straight diagonal line to the pyramid with the "X."

"X marks the spot," was the family joke.

The problem was "Dumas is your key." The word "Dumas" did not translate. There was no French word for "Dumas" other than the name of the French author.

Joseph became convinced the answer must have had something to do with the author, Alexandre Dumas. After all, his father was a general in Napoleon Bonaparte's army. Looking for some sort of clue, Joseph read everything Dumas had written from *The Count of Monte Cristo* to *The Three Musketeers*. He even read the more obscure plays Dumas had written. He found no clue.

For years, Joseph struggled with the "Dumas" problem. Anagrams provided nothing in French or English. He even tried Spanish, but there was no translation for "Dumas." "Who or what was Dumas? What kind of key am I looking for? Where is the key hidden? A key to what: a door, a box, the medallion? How can you have a key to a medallion?"

The answer was remarkably simple once he accidentally figured out what it was.

It had come to him almost four years ago while reading a biography of Benjamin Franklin. The "Dumas key" was a cipher, a famous cipher at that. One used quite frequently during the American Revolution.

Apparently, the founding fathers had utilized a number of ciphers in their correspondence to protect their war plans in case letters fell into the hands of the British. The most famous of these ciphers was created by Charles William Fredrick Dumas.

Benjamin Franklin himself had used the Dumas cipher in his letters while he was the American Representative to the French Court during the American Revolution.

Benton knew that while in France, Franklin lived in the home of Count de Chaumont at Passy, and it was the Count's son who'd sold the land in upstate New York to his royal ancestor.

When Benton read about the cipher in Franklin's biography, he wondered if it could be that simple. It had only taken a few minutes on the internet to find it.

Dumas' cipher is a heavily homophonic simple substitution system. Each letter is enciphered as a number from 1 to 682 ("simple substitution"). Most letters have many numbers assigned to it ("heavily homophonic") and any one of such assigned numbers may be used. Thus, "BED" can be enciphered as "118 5 20" but there are numerous other ways to represent "BED" such as "163 13 325", "118 13 20", etc. Besides alphabetical letters, the table includes such symbols as the ampersand (&), the apostrophe ('), the comma (,), the interrogation (?), the full stop (.), the division or hyphen (=), and the reference (*).

The website even included an enciphering table. The numbers around the edge of the medallion could be translated with a simple substitution cipher. It didn't take more than an hour to figure it out.

Snowshoe River | 2 falls | 125° | 5 miles.

After thirty years of research, it was an enormous breakthrough.

However, a new problem presented itself. Where is Snowshoe River? Joseph Benton knew the Adirondacks well but he had never heard of a Snowshoe River. He had gone over every topographic map of the region, inch by inch, and could not find a Snowshoe River anywhere. He had read every history book about the area, including several out-of-print books at local historical societies.

They offered nothing.

It had been a lonely search. Over the past 30 years Joseph often was saddened that he had no one to share his research with. His ex-wife, Sharon, thought he was crazy spending so much time on such nonsense. He always wished he had a sibling he could bounce ideas off. Two minds are better than one, he thought. He would gladly have shared the treasure.

As he pondered over the mysterious Snowshoe River, Joseph had often thought of asking his friend Jerry about it. Jerry was as good a friend as anybody could ever hope for. He was there all during Joseph's divorce and always seemed to know the right thing to say. They had been best friends for years and Jerry certainly knew about Joseph's heritage and the legend. He and Joseph often joked about it, but it was never clear that Jerry thought there might be any truth to the wild stories. Jerry was too grounded to believe such things, but he understood why Joseph's marriage had failed. Still, he had no idea how consumed Joseph really was with the legend.

It would be another year before Joseph discovered the location of Snowshoe River.

The second epiphany came while he was reading *Adirondack Life* magazine. An ad caught his eye: snowshoes made by the Raquette River Snowshoe Company. It hit him: *raquette* means snowshoe in French.

"The Raquette River! How could I have missed it?"

He was getting close to his goal. He could feel it. Find the two falls on the Raquette River, take a compass heading of 125° and go five miles. He smiled to himself, "X marks the spot."

Back to the topographic maps, he now was searching for two falls on the Raquette River. He reminded himself that King Bonaparte hid the treasure in the 1830s, before dams were built on the river. The Raquette River now had dozens of dams. In the 1830s, there had been falls and rapids all along the river that ran from Raquette Lake in Hamilton County, north to its outlet in the St. Lawrence River just east of Massena. "Which two falls?" he asked himself. There were hundreds.

The Raquette River was about 60 miles east of Lake Bonaparte, only 20 miles from Benton's home in Cranberry Lake. It was time for another road trip.

That afternoon, with topographic maps and compass on the seat beside him, he followed State Highway 3 east toward the river, along what would have been little more than a dirt trail 180 years ago. Where the highway crossed the river near Piercefield, there were two dams. Setting Pole Dam and the Piercefield hydroelectric dam were less than three miles apart. These had to be the two falls, he thought. It would make sense since this road would have been the only trail from Lake Bonaparte to the Raquette River at the time. He checked the map and knew he was right. In the 1830s the area would have matched perfectly the map at the center of the medallion.

He'd found it!

Joseph remembered that feeling of excitement, just one year before the divorce, when he got out of the car at the parking area by the Piercefield Dam. After 30 years he was so close. It took only a few minutes to find a spot where he could get a good compass reading with a clear view to the south and east, 125°.

He looked at the compass, looked up, looked at the compass again.

When he finally looked up again, he instantly knew what he was looking at: Big Tupper Ski Area on Mt. Morris, just outside the Village of Tupper Lake. It could be seen for miles and was unmistakable because of the long vertical clearings on the side of the mountain—the ski trails. This time of year they were still white with snow.

The bible map was incredibly easy, yet its meaning had remained hidden for more than 180 years.

Joseph was now convinced he knew where the Spanish Royal Treasure was buried. It must be somewhere on the property of the Big Tupper Ski Area. And, that was precisely why he'd invested two million dollars of his family fortune in the Adirondack Mountain & Lake Resort. The Resort was a six-thousand-acre development planned for the Big Tupper property. Designed as a "Year Round Community" with hotels, condos, single family homes, and Adirondack Great Camps, Joseph figured his investment would give him access to the property before construction began, and before some construction worker accidentally found the treasure.

Because the Resort was within the "Blue Line" that defined the park, the Adirondack Park Agency controlled the permit process. Enshrined in the New York State Constitution in 1892, the Adirondack Park was the largest area of protected land in the lower forty-eight states—over six million acres. It's larger than the Yellowstone, Everglades, Glacier, and Grand Canyon National Parks combined.

Within the boundary of the park, nearly half of the land belongs to the people of New York State and is constitutionally protected to remain a "Forever Wild" forest preserve. The remaining half of the park is private land and includes farms, timberlands, businesses, homes, and camps. The APA has tight control over development of these private lands.

Because of the size of the project, the Resort had become one of the biggest public controversies in the Adirondacks. Tupper Lake residents, for the most part, supported the project because of the economic impact it would have on their community. Joseph now worried about the economic impact the project might have on him. He might be about to lose his two million dollars. The decision next week by Judge Kelly regarding the future of the Resort could very well determine his future. Finding the Spanish Royal Treasure had suddenly become critical to his financial solvency. He was getting desperate.

Joseph wished there was some way he could delay the hearing next week. He was still trying to decide what outcome would best suit his interest.

If Judge Kelly rules in favor of the Resort, as a major investor, Joseph would have access to the property. The problem with this outcome was hundreds of construction workers would also have access to the property. And, they had earth moving equipment. They could accidentally stumble across the treasure while cutting roads or digging foundations.

Several months ago he had struck up a relationship with the executive director of Adirondack Environmental Watch. He thought at the time she may somehow be a help. Not a direct help in finding the treasure, because he'd never intended to tell her about it. But, maybe he could use her influence. If nothing else he could keep track of the lawsuit from the inside.

Deep down he didn't like the deception in this new relationship, but he reminded himself, "desperate times require desperate measures." Joseph grinned, "These desperate measures had some great benefits."

Joseph knew the treasure was somewhere on the Big Tupper property, but he still didn't know where on the property it was. He had spent many a lonely hour over the past three years roaming the six-thousand-acre property with a metal detector. He had gotten hits in a number of areas that needed further exploration. The problem had been Judge Kelly's "shovel ruling," an injunction that absolutely forbade any digging on the property until final permits were issued. One thing he learned from his lady friend was that Adirondack Environmental Watch activists were watching the property for violations of the shovel ruling. He didn't dare risk pursuing any of his leads. Anyway, he didn't have earth moving equipment and never even brought a shovel with him on his search.

If the judge allowed the Resort to move forward, he just might be able to use some of the construction equipment that certainly would be spread around the property. It would be a race to see who found the treasure first, an accidental find by a construction worker or Joseph.

On the other hand, if the judge ruled against the Resort, the developers would abandon the project. He'd lose every penny of his investment and be ruined financially. However, it would also mean he would have access to the property without any interference. He knew the treasure was there somewhere, and it could easily be worth several hundred times his two-million-dollar investment.

While Joseph had options either way, he still felt the need to try to influence the judge's decision one way or another. He just wasn't sure which way.

For now, his best short term outcome would be to delay the hearing, but how?

FOUR

ALICIA LACROIX was looking forward to meeting her new adversary. She mused on the fifteen-minute drive from her office in Ray Brook to the Crowne Plaza Hotel in Lake Placid that the Resort had chosen a woman to be their project manager. She was intrigued . . . not really surprised, but definitely intrigued.

As she approached her table by the window with a lovely view of Mirror Lake and the high peaks of the Adirondacks, anyone might have mistaken her for a fashion model or a high level businesswoman, rather than an environmental activist. Moreover, she was not opposed to using her long blond hair and fit good looks to her advantage whenever she thought it would help. She was a radical activist more than a feminist. That was obvious by the various ways she dressed. Some days she would be in a designer business suit, other days you could find her in tight jeans and t-shirt, whatever suited her purpose.

Alicia watched as a number of people entered the restaurant. A few women entered alone but she knew they weren't McCalister. She had a gut feeling what McCalister looked like just from their short phone conversation. It was a game she played, guessing what people looked like before she met them. She was actually quite good at it.

Finally, at 12:17 p.m. a tallish woman walked through the door and Alicia knew immediately this was her luncheon appointment. She stood and raised her hand above her head. Maureen McCalister saw her, nodded and walked over to the table.

After a brief handshake both women sat and made themselves comfortable.

Maureen deliberately did not apologize for being late. Let the games begin, she thought to herself.

"How was your trip to the Adirondacks?"

"It was an uneventful drive, but some of the most beautiful scenery in America. I think I'm going to like it here."

"This is the gloomy time, wait until the leaves are on the trees. Fall is the most beautiful time here." As she said this, Alicia was thinking, of course, she won't even last till the fall. Too bad she'll never get to see it.

The small talk lasted through the meal. Maureen thought Alicia looked tired. They both had the arugula salad with apple slices, pan-seared perch with saffron rice, and a glass of white wine.

Alicia gave a very brief history of her six years in the Adirondacks and McCalister talked about her husband and two boys and how they were going to love it here. Knowing full well it would turn Alicia's stomach, Maureen went into detail about her husband's love of hunting and how he was looking forward to spending quality time with the boys teaching them the sport.

She could see Alicia's face change as she went on about hunting. Maureen also knew that Alicia knew what she was doing.

This was a game. They both knew it.

Neither ordered desert. Over coffee, Maureen thought to herself for the second time today, "Showtime."

"So Alicia, tell me, how do you think next week's hearing is going to go?"

"Well, it's been a long haul," LaCroix began cautiously. "Everybody is tired of this case. Judge Kelly has signaled to both sides he's prepared to make a final decision."

"I haven't been here twenty-four hours yet. Any idea which way he's going to go?"

Alicia smiled, "If I knew, I'm not sure I'd tell you."

Maureen smiled back, "Of course not. Shane Baxter, our attorney, told me he talked to Judge Kelly's clerk yesterday trying to feel him out. He apparently didn't get anything"

"I'm not surprised," Alicia said. "I talked to the clerk myself this morning. Brendan Martin is his name. He recently graduated from Georgetown. He's a sharp kid. He told me he was working on a draft order for the judge, but frankly didn't give me any idea at all which way the judge was leaning. By the way, I like Shane. He is a very good lawyer, you're lucky to have him."

"Thank you, we like him." More gamesmanship, Maureen thought.

A bit surprised about the draft ruling, Maureen had to ask, "Is it common for a judge to have a ruling written before the final arguments?"

"Actually, it's not unusual at all in a big case. After all, Judge Kelly has been working on this case for almost ten years. He's seen dozens of briefs from both sides. He's read thousands of pages of expert testimony and environmental studies. He's heard oral arguments from both sides. I think he's ready for the case to go away. No doubt he has made his decision, pending any major surprises next week. You're not planning a major surprise are you?"

Maureen laughed, "I don't think so, are you?"

"Hardly."

"Alicia, let me be frank. The Adirondack Mountain & Lake Resort has gone beyond all reasonable efforts, investing millions to protect the land, groundwater and wildlife. We have changed our design significantly because of your suggestions. In short, we have done everything your organization has asked. This is the most environmentally sound development project in America. You know that! Why are we still here? Not to be disrespectful, but any further arguments by your side are absolutely absurd."

Alicia LaCroix thought for a moment. Her anger was building at Maureen's brashness and she didn't want to show her hand. Then it just came out.

"You are so naïve, Mrs. McCalister. First of all, you have done everything we have asked except one thing: putting an end to this development for good. Let me explain this to you as simply as I can. You're in the Adirondacks now, and while your activities may be rural, your problems are urban. You may be saving a few trees in your project, but we have the votes. Your problem is what the public and the APA *think* you are doing in these woods, accurate or inaccurate. And, they *think* what I tell them to think. Unlike you, I have no ethical or moral code I have to adhere to. Developers like you exist for profit. Because of that, you are immediately suspect, regardless of the merits of your dear project. Environmentalists like me are seen as proponents of the common good, regardless of the absurdity of our arguments. It's profit-mad developers like you, verses tree hugging little old ladies in aprons. In the court of public opinion, you lose every time, and I predict you are going to lose next week in the court of law as well. Thank you for lunch . . . good day, Mrs. McCalister." Alicia LaCroix got up and stormed out of the Crowne Plaza.

"Wow, she is a bitch. I never said anything about buying lunch. That was quite a display of political theater," Maureen thought as she paid the bill. "She's a good actress as well."

Truthfully, Maureen was quite pleased with herself for eliciting

Alicia's little tirade. She reached into her purse, took out the digital recorder and switched it off.

On her way back to the office she made two stops. The first was a bookstore on Main Street in Lake Placid, where she bought a copy of *The Art of War* for Shane Baxter. The second stop was T. F. Finnigan's Men's Shop on Main Street in Saranac Lake.

FIVE

ORGANIZED CHAOS is an oxymoron, but it was an apt description of the offices of the Administrative Law Court in Ray Brook, New York, housed in a large complex of single story state government buildings.

The court itself consists of only two judges, a clerk and a secretary. Judge Noah Pennington, III, was the Senior Judge, but it was Judge Robert Kelly who had the biggest case.

APA cases typically took up most of the court's docket, and *Adirondack Environmental Watch, et al v. Adirondack Mountain & Lake Resort* was the mother of all APA cases.

Law clerk Brendan Martin had been putting the finishing touches on the draft of Judge Kelly's final ruling. Tired of the daily calls from all parties, Brendan was glad the Resort case would finally be coming to an end. "Thank goodness I haven't been here for the whole thing," he would say. The judge often reminded Brendan he'd been only sixteen years old when the case started.

"Any word?" He called out to the secretary.

"Not yet. Patience is a virtue, Brendan."

An eager young clerk, only a year out of law school, Brendan was anxious to have Judge Kelly review the draft brief. It was two p.m. and the judge hadn't come to work yet today. He hadn't even called. Brendan was beginning to worry that the judge would soon arrive and want to go over the first set of revisions late into the evening.

"I hope he's not going to want to work tonight, my Hoyas are playing at seven."

Val, the secretary, yelled back "I didn't even know you had Hoyas. You're only 26."

Brendan shook his head smiling. It was the third week of March, and Georgetown was playing in the first round of the NCAA tournament.

"Does Judge Pennington know you have Hoyas at your tender age?"

"No he doesn't. I never told him for fear he'd have me arrested. By the way, you better be careful Val, my Hoyas can be contagious."

As Senior Judge, Pennington was really Brendan's boss, but the vast amount of work he did was for Judge Kelly. Judge Pennington was a graduate of Syracuse University. Syracuse was also in the tournament.

Val hadn't gone to Syracuse University, but she was a native of Syracuse and a loyal fan. "Don't worry Bren, I'm immune, my blood flows orange. And no, he hasn't called yet."

Val had been secretary for the Administrative Law Court for thirty-two years. Hired by Judge Pennington when the court was first set up in Ray Brook, she was looking at retirement in just two years.

While she had not said anything to Brendan, Val was a little worried that they had not heard from Judge Kelly this late in the day. When she'd talked to Judge Pennington earlier, she'd asked him if Judge Kelly had said anything about his plans for today. Pennington told her that he had talked to Judge Kelly yesterday and all he'd said was that, except for Friday, the rest of the week was dedicated to finishing the final orders in the Resort case. He hadn't mentioned whether he'd be in the office today or not.

Val had thought of calling the Kelly home, but Mrs. Kelly was recovering from breast cancer surgery and had recently started chemotherapy. She really didn't want to bother either of them, particularly if Mrs. Kelly was having a bad day. On the other hand it was quite unusual for the judge not to call.

Just as she was getting ready to dial, the phone rang.

"Val, it's Sadie Kelly, is Bob available?"

"The judge hasn't been here all day, Mrs. Kelly. I thought he was home with you. Are you okay?"

"I'm fine," there was a short pause, "but now I'm worried. He didn't come home last night. I know he was working late on that Resort case and I just thought he'd worked all night. He hasn't done that in years, but it's happened. I've been waiting for his call all day."

"We haven't heard from him either. I've been getting worried too. I thought maybe he was home with you."

"Where could he be, Val?"

"I have no idea. Let me make a few calls and I'll get back to you. Maybe he did work all night and was too tired to drive home. If he got a room for the night, he might still be sleeping."

"I'm worried, Val."

"Don't worry Mrs. Kelly. I'm sure he's just fine. I'll get back to you in a few minutes."

Val knew that if Judge Kelly stayed over in town it would be at the Crowne Plaza. There was no way he'd stay in any of the low-end motels that dotted the highway between Saranac Lake and Lake Placid. She made the call and the day manager told her the judge had not registered at the hotel last night.

Val's hands had begun to shake. She called Brendan over to her desk and told him about her last two conversations. "I was sure he'd be at the Crowne Plaza. Bren, what do you think we should do now? Should I call the state police? I really don't want to call Mrs. Kelly back without knowing anything."

"I'll call Judge Pennington and let him know what's going on. We'll figure this out." With a wink he added, "Remember Val, patience is a virtue."

Brendan got Judge Pennington on the line in the courthouse in Malone, the Franklin County seat, where he'd been hearing a small civil case because all the local judges were either busy or had conflicts. "Judge, we don't know where to go from here and Val doesn't want to call Mrs. Kelly back without any answers. Could you call her?"

"Okay Brendan, I'll call her on my way back to the office. Meanwhile, call the state police and have them meet me at the office. I should be there in just over an hour."

"Okay Judge, we'll see you then. If we hear anything before you get here, I'll call."

"Thanks. And Brendan, keep Val calm, she has a tendency to get a bit hysterical at times like this. In fact, maybe you should just send her home and tell her we'll call her with updates."

"Yes sir, you drive safe Judge."

Brendan truly enjoyed working for these two judges. Both had been caring mentors. He often thought he'd learned more in one year working for these two men than three years of law school. Both Judges had Brendan to their homes for dinner many times. Their wives loved to dote over him. Sometimes it made him feel like a little kid again. It sure made it easier being away from his family and his girlfriend. He had come to really appreciate and care for both these men and their wives.

After crossing his heart and double promising to call, he finally convinced Val to go home. Then he called the state police, whose barracks were only a few hundred yards down the road. They said someone would be by shortly.

Brendan took a few minutes to check Judge Kelly's office to see if he could tell how much progress the judge had made on the final ruling. Alone in the office, he tried not to think the worst, but the longer he was alone, the more he worried. Growing up, he often thought the worst and his parents would frequently urge him to be more optimistic. "Stop projecting negative thoughts," he could hear his mom telling him.

He had been in deep thought for almost twenty minutes and was startled by the door opening. A burly, no-neck state trooper came lumbering in. He put his hat on Val's desk and introduced himself. Still a bit dazed, Brendan introduced himself. "I'm sorry, I didn't get your name."

"Trooper Mike Murphy."

"Thanks for getting here so quickly. Judge Pennington should be here any minute."

"So what's going on?" Murphy asked, "Something about a missing person?"

Brendan was explaining the situation when Judge Pennington came in. He finished his explanation by saying that it didn't look as if Judge Kelly had worked all night. In fact, it didn't appear he had even gotten through much of what Brendan had left for him yesterday to review.

Judge Pennington was an elegant looking man with his silver hair and beard and grey wool suit. Murphy could see the concern in Pennington's face. A soft-spoken man, the judge told Murphy he had just gotten off the phone with Mrs. Kelly. She still hadn't heard from her husband and was worried sick.

Murphy asked Judge Pennington if there was anyone who could stay with Mrs. Kelly for a while. The Judge called his wife while Trooper Murphy phoned the station commander, Sergeant Sam Perry, to bring him up to date. Murphy requested a female trooper go out to talk with Mrs. Kelly while he completed statements with the judge and the clerk at the court.

The sergeant instructed Murphy to kill time with small talk until another trooper joined him at the court. They'd then separate the judge and the law clerk and get detailed statements. After all, it was a missing judge. "We'll be careful and do this one by the book, just in case."

It was after five when the second trooper arrived. Judge Pennington and Brendan understood what was happening and appreciated the professionalism and caution. By then, both were silently afraid of what might have happened to their friend and colleague.

SIX

MAUREEN MCCALISTER arrived back at her Tupper Lake office around three thirty carrying two small shopping bags and a hanging vinyl bag on a wooden coat hanger. She was pleased with her purchases.

She stopped at the receptionist's desk and smiled at the young man on the phone. The Resort even had a male receptionist. Actually, he was an all around errand boy, but answering the phones was one of his main duties.

He immediately finished his call and hung up the phone. "Can I help you Mrs. McCalister?"

"Thanks Tommy, and please, call me Maureen. Could you put these things in my office? I want to freshen up."

"Sure thing Mrs. McCal . . . I mean Maureen. Were my directions okay?"

"Perfect. I found everything with no problem. Thanks. Oh, could you please tell Shane I'm back and ready to meet with him?"

"Sure thing. By the way, I cleaned the restroom for you. It was pretty grungy with just us guys working here. We'd been using both the men's and the ladies'."

"Thanks Tommy."

"Great," she thought. "This should be interesting."

Actually, the restroom sparkled and even had a lavender air freshener hidden somewhere. There was a single fresh green carnation on the edge of the wash basin. St. Patrick's Day, she remembered.

She reminded herself to thank Tommy for his thoughtfulness.

Two fresh flower arrangements greeted her in her office. On the desk were a dozen red roses with a sweet note from her husband and boys wishing her well her first day on the job. The credenza displayed a huge arrangement from the home office, welcoming her to the Adirondack Mountain & Lake Resort team.

"Knock'em dead," the note said.

The mahogany desk and credenza dominated the spacious office. A round conference table and four leather chairs were in one corner by a window, and a six foot square scale model of the proposed development in the another corner.

Shane Baxter stuck his head around the corner and gave a soft tap on the door, "Ready to talk?" He joined Maureen at the conference table.

Baxter was a thirty-two-year-old Columbia Law School graduate with a remarkable reputation as a trial lawyer. At Columbia, he'd been editor of the *Law Review* and had won every moot court award the school had to offer.

On the table were the two shopping bags. One from The Bookstore Plus, the other from T. F. Finnigan's Men's Shop. On the coat rack was the hanging bag.

"I come from the East bearing gifts," Maureen said.

"Surely you're not suggesting I'm the messiah."

Maureen laughed. "If we win this case next week you'll be a god in my book."

"I thought gifts came after we won the case."

"Not this time. These gifts are going to help you win the case."

"Really. I thought it was my brilliant mind, hard work and youthful good looks that were going to win the case."

"Whoever said you were good looking? Was someone trying to get you into bed? Not even your mother would have told you that."

Actually, Maureen thought Shane was a very good looking man. If I were twenty years younger and single, I might even be interested, she thought.

"Thanks for the compliment boss."

"My pleasure, I'm full of them."

"Now there's that sweet personality I heard so much about."

"Speaking of sweet personalities, Ms. Bitch had very nice things to say about you at lunch. She said we're lucky to have you. She's right, we are lucky to have you. She also told me she spoke to Judge Kelly's clerk this morning and he was putting the final touches on the judge's orders."

"I'm not surprised. I'm sure she also told you what was in those orders."

"No, she kept that to herself."

"So what did you think of her?"

"The 'Ms. Bitch' moniker is overly kind. She had a hissy fit and stormed out of the restaurant after lunch . . . and left me with the bill."

"Do tell."

"We'll talk about that later. First, I want a brief summary of where we stand for next week."

Shane Baxter wore a dark blue custom-tailored, pinstriped suit, with a pink and black striped silk tie and matching solid pink handkerchief in the jacket pocket.

"I think we're actually in good shape," he explained. "The environmental studies we submitted to the court counter everything they submitted. We've shown tremendous flexibility and willingness to adjust our plans based on some of their concerns. The APA staff has even privately complemented us. Ricky Hartman, the APA director, still sides with Ms. Bitch, but there's nothing we can do about that. Our environmental studies have been reviewed by three different university professors and their testimony is some of the strongest evidence we've introduced. Their cross examination of our witnesses actually hurt them. Our cross examination of their witnesses showed some flaws in their impact studies. On Monday, both sides will summarize their case and we wait for the judge to make his decision. I suspect he'll rule from the bench on Monday, and within a week or two, we'll have written orders."

"What happens if we win?"

"Ms. Bitch will shit her pants right there in the courtroom, and then she'll ask the judge to enjoin his ruling until appeals can be heard. Another two years of legal wrangling."

"What will the judge do then?"

Shane smiled, "After asking Ms. Bitch to clean up her own mess, I have absolutely no idea."

"I have two final questions. Have you written your final summation yet? And, can new evidence be introduced next week?"

"I've got the first draft of my final arguments right here." He knew she would be asking and handed her a copy. "But, it would be highly unusual to introduce new evidence at a final hearing. I would have to let the judge and the plaintiffs know right away. Depending on what it is, Ms. Bitch will fight it, and who knows what the APA would do. If it's pertinent, after all is said and done, I think we could convince the judge to allow it. Why do you ask?"

"I'll get to that in a minute. First, the gifts."

She picked up the bookstore bag and took out a copy of *The Art of War* and handed it to Shane.

"This was written twenty-five hundred years ago. It's maybe the best business strategy book ever written. I want you to take tomorrow morning off and read it. When you finish, you may want to make some changes to your final arguments."

Making a nod to the papers Shane had given her, she added, "I'll wait and read the revised version of your summation."

"Thanks. I think."

"Now, young good looking man, what size slacks and sport coat do you wear?"

"Isn't that kind of personal?" Shane was kidding, but he wasn't sure where this conversation was going.

"Come on. Tell me."

"I'm a 42 long, a 34" waist, and 33" length slacks. Why?"

"Wow, I'm good." Maureen said.

"What do you mean?"

"Are you familiar with the phrase, when in Rome . . . ?"

"Sure."

"You agree with it, right?"

"I guess."

Maureen got up, went to the coat rack, pulled down the hanger and unzipped the bag. Out came a camelhair sport coat and brown wool slacks.

"What's that?"

"You're not as smart a lawyer as I thought. This is a jacket and a pair of slacks."

Shane rolled his eyes.

"I want you to wear this in court on Monday. The jacket size and slacks waist are perfect. You'll have to have the slacks shortened though, I thought you were taller. I saw a tailor on Main Street. He can do it while you wait. I even got you a silk bow tie."

She opened the other bag on the table and pulled out a red, green and beige plaid bow tie.

"I'm supposed to look like a clown?"

"No Shane. You're in Rome. Here you look like a clown in the getup you're in now. This is the Adirondacks, man. Pinstriped suits don't fit; especially custom-tailored pinstriped suits . . . forgive the pun."

"Whatever you say. But I don't know how to tie that silly tie. I'll wear one of my own."

"I'll have Tommy get on the internet and print you directions. You'll figure it out. Now, if you're finished complaining about the nice clothes I bought you, I have one more gift."

"I can't wait."

Maureen got up again and went to her desk. From a bottom drawer she took out her purse. She reached in and pulled out a digital recorder the size of a pack of cigarettes. Maureen knew that as long as one party was aware the recording was taking place, it was completely legal in New York State.

"I want you to listen to this. I think you'll like this present best."

Maureen had already fast forwarded past the small talk during lunch and started playing the conversation that had taken place over coffee. Her face beamed as they both listened intently.

Shane appeared shocked as he listened. "I can't believe she said those things to you."

"*No* ethical or moral code! Proponents of the common good, *regardless* of the absurdity of her arguments! The APA thinks what *she* tells them to think!"

"I'll tell you what I think," Shane said.

"What's that?"

"Ms. Bitch will do everything in her power to not allow this on the record and, after hearing it, I can assure you, the APA will fight it too. That being said, I still think we can get it in. Judge Kelly would love to hear this. This must be why you asked if we could introduce new evidence? Why didn't you tell me this morning you were going to record your conversation with Ms. Bitch?"

"If I had told you, what would you have said?"

"Don't do it!"

"Exactly. Fight fire with fire," she said.

"Fire with fire," he repeated with a big smile. "I think I'll enjoy reading this book tomorrow."

"I think you will," she said, handing him the recorder. "Now get out of here, I have some real work to do."

As he was leaving the office with his presents in hand, Shane turned around, "You're a scary woman Mrs. McCalister, I'm sure glad we're on the same side. I'll wear the bow tie."

SEVEN

TROOPER MURPHY was interviewing Judge Pennington in his office and Trooper Schalit, who had just arrived, was talking with Brendan at a table in the front of the courtroom. Neither Judge Pennington nor Brendan were considered suspects, but it was standard procedure to separate possible witnesses when taking their statements. Judge Kelly's wife was giving a statement to Trooper Susan LaFrance, who had been sent to her home.

The questions for all three were basically the same. "When was the last time you saw Judge Kelly? Was he having any personal problems? Was he having an affair? What kind of cases was he working on? Was he depressed? Do you know anybody who would want to hurt him? Was it his habit to make any stops on his way home? How much alcohol did he drink? What kind of car did he drive? Did he have any medical problems?"

When asked about his whereabouts the previous night, Judge Pennington told Murphy that Monday was poker night, and he and four friends had played from seven to eleven p.m. at his house. His wife was there as well. Brendan told Trooper Schalit he was home alone watching ESPN and the pre-game predictions for the basketball tournament.

As for the rest of the questions, all three gave basically the same answers. Judge Kelly had a rock-solid marriage with three kids and seven grandchildren. Even after thirty-three years of marriage, he absolutely worshiped Mrs. Kelly, and never even looked at another woman. The thought of an affair was nonsense. He had no enemies. Since he was a judge for the Administrative Court, he did not hear criminal cases, and parties in administrative cases aren't known for criminal behavior, especially foul play.

An avid fisherman and hunter, he had a zest for life, particularly the outdoors. In fact, just yesterday morning when asked how he was, he'd responded, "It's a brand new unused Monday morning. Life is great!" He then added, "If you're too busy to go fishing then you're just too darn busy." He was looking forward to the opening of trout season in a few weeks. The Resort case would be over by then, and he had already planned on taking a few days off to go fishing with a few friends.

Mrs. Kelly did tell Trooper LaFrance that she had talked to her husband about nine thirty last night. He explained he was working late on the final orders in the big case he was hearing. He suggested she go to bed and said he would be home in a couple of hours. "That was the last time I spoke with him." With tears in her eyes, she also told the trooper he did have a habit of stopping at the convenience store down the road from the office to pick up a bottle of orange soda for the ride home. Orange soda was one of his few obsessions. Other than an occasional glass of white wine, he rarely drank alcohol. He had no serious medical problems. "Noah is a good man," she said.

Judge Kelly drove a black, 2011 Range Rover. This information was called in to the station commander as soon as the interviews were complete. An alert was sent to all troopers in the area to keep their eyes open for the vehicle.

Trooper Murphy asked Judge Pennington if he would develop a list of the cases Judge Kelly had been involved with for the past five years. He also wanted the names of the parties in each case, with contact information. The Judge said Val could have the list available by noon tomorrow.

Murphy said he'd be by to pick it up. He wanted to talk to Val anyway. Maybe she had some additional information.

Murphy also took a look in Judge Kelly's office without touching anything. He saw nothing unusual, although he did ask Judge Pennington to lock the door and ordered no one to go in until a team from the Forensic Investigative Unit completed their work. After that, Brendan and Val would be asked to inventory the office to see if any documents were missing. Judge Kelly rarely took work home, the trooper was told. He preferred to work late in the office. That way he maintained a complete separation of home and office.

Judge Kelly lived in a lakefront home on Corey's Road about twenty minutes west of Saranac Lake, just off Route 3. It was almost seven p.m. when Trooper LaFrance finished her interview with Mrs. Kelly. The change to daylight saving time was just a week ago so there still was a little daylight left. La France knew that in a missing person case, the first thing suspected is an accident while driving home. On her way back to the Ray Brook barracks, LaFrance drove slowly to check for any sign that a vehicle might have driven off the side of the road. Over the years she had seen a number of accidents along this part of the highway with its deep ravines and water. She knew if the judge had gone off the road, it wouldn't necessarily be obvious. She also knew this time of year there were more accidents with deer. The station commander had already ordered another trooper to drive the route looking for the same thing. If nothing turned up tonight, this procedure would be repeated again tomorrow when the light was better.

Back in Ray Brook, Trooper LaFrance stopped at the three convenience stores closest to the judge's office to see if anyone had seen him last night. The first two didn't know the judge and didn't remember seeing anyone matching his description, or even buying an orange soda for that matter. Both cashiers reported that orange soda was not a particularly popular item. The cashier in the third store knew Judge Kelly well. He got most of his gas there, and he almost always bought an orange soda as well. No one had seen him yesterday.

A routine call to the Adirondack Medical Center Hospital in Saranac Lake provided nothing.

Mrs. Kelly's thoughts were spinning when Trooper LaFrance left. She was having a hard time not crying. All she could think was, "Where could he be? Is he hurt?" The interview had been difficult for her. While Judge Pennington's wife was there to provide comfort, the questions regarding possible affairs and depression were weighing on her. Judge Kelly did own a number of handguns and rifles, but a quick inventory showed all were accounted for. He never carried a weapon with him unless he was hunting.

Mrs. Kelly called her three children to let them know what was happening. Their oldest son, Bob, Jr., lived in Albany and promised to be there first thing in the morning. If he left at five a.m. he would be there shortly after eight. The other two children lived in Boston and Portland, Maine, and promised they would talk again tomorrow.

Before he left the office to head to the Kelly home, Judge Pennington called the state police station commander, and asked if all this could be kept out of the papers, for a while at least. Sergeant Perry promised nothing would be released tonight, but could not make any commitment beyond that. Pennington thanked him and they agreed to talk tomorrow.

Brendan called to update Val, as promised, then went directly home. He no longer had any interest in watching the basketball game. I'll get the score from the paper tomorrow, he thought. He made himself a sandwich, grabbed a beer, and went in to lie on the bed. He never even turned the lights on. He just thought about Judge and Mrs. Kelly and how kind they both had been to him. He said a prayer for the Kellys and went to sleep.

Judge Pennington left for the Kelly home to join his wife. On his drive, he mentally reviewed the cases on Judge Kelly's docket. He made a mental note to sit with Val and Brendan first thing in the morning to decide what should be done with each case, at least for the next few weeks.

After finally convincing Mrs. Kelly to lie down, Judge Pennington and his wife sat in the Kelly living room and shared with each other the events of the evening. Mrs. Pennington had promised to spend the night in the guest room. The two quietly talked about what might have happened to their friend. It was difficult to come up with an explanation that had a positive ending. Neither had a good feeling about what was happening.

EIGHT

JOSEPH BENTON woke at six thirty a.m. After feeding Bailey, he sat down and was watching the news with his morning coffee when he saw a reporter doing a stand-up from the Tampa International Airport:

> *The planet's northern magnetic pole is drifting slowly but steadily towards Russia—and it's throwing off planes in Florida.*
>
> *"Tampa International Airport was forced to readjust its runway numbers Thursday to account for the movement of the earth's magnetic field. This is information that pilots rely on to navigate planes. Thanks to the fluctuations in the magnetic field, the airport has closed its primary runway until March 22 to change taxiway signs to account for this shift, the Federal Aviation Administration told us.*

Joseph knew the numbers painted on the end of runways were actually compass headings to guide pilots. The news story continued with a spokesman for the FAA:

> *The magnetic poles are generated by movements within the earth's inner and outer cores, though the exact process isn't understood. They're constantly in flux, moving a few degrees every year, but the changes are almost never of such a magnitude*

that runways require adjusting,

He couldn't believe what he was hearing. A shift in compass headings! That could mean his "walks" in the Big Tupper Ski area with his metal detector were probably nowhere near where the treasure was actually buried. King Joseph's compass heading from the 1830s could be way off today. I've been looking in the wrong place, he thought. On his walks, Benton had gotten a number of hits from the detector, but none of the magnitude he would have expected.

Joseph refilled his coffee and sat at the computer. He typed "magnetic shift" in Google and thousands of hits appeared.

The first site he visited was the Geological Survey of Canada.

Scientists have long known that the magnetic pole moves. James Ross located the magnetic pole for the first time in 1831 after an exhausting arctic journey during which his ship got stuck in the ice for four years. No one returned until the next century. In 1904, Roald Amundsen found the pole again and discovered that it had moved—at least 50 km since the days of Ross.

The pole kept moving north during the 20th century, at an average speed of 10 km per year, lately accelerating to 40 km per year. At this rate it will exit North America and reach Siberia in a few decades.

Keeping track of the north magnetic pole today is Larry Newitt's job with the Geological Survey of Canada. "We usually go out and check its location once every few years," he says. "We'll have to make more trips now that it is moving so quickly."

Earth's magnetic field is changing in other ways, too:

Compass needles in Africa have been drifting about 1 degree per decade. And globally, the magnetic field has weakened 10% since the 19th century.

"One degree per decade," Joseph said to himself. He did the math. "That's an 18 degree difference from 1830. If that's accurate, I'm way, way off."

On the internet there was also a news story from the *Tampa-St. Petersburg Times* that had the same information as the story he's just seen on TV. Another news site talked about the fact that the change in magnetic north was something pilots and sailors have known about for years. Now their digital navigation equipment calculates the change automatically.

He checked a few other sites. One thing he learned was that the exact degree of change in compass headings depends on location. The one degree per decade shift in compass headings in Africa may be very different than the shift in Tupper Lake. Joseph decided he needed help figuring out exactly what the difference was in Tupper Lake between 1830 and today.

He noticed that most of the experts referred to in the websites he visited were geologists or geophysicists. He needed one.

It didn't take long to find the e-mail address for Dr. Nathanael Rutland, Chairman of the Geology Department at Rensselaer Polytechnic Institute in Troy, New York. Dr. Rutland himself specialized in metamorphic petrology, "whatever that is," Joseph muttered to himself.

He drafted a letter saying he was an author writing a treasure hunt novel, and was looking for help with magnetic north declination differences from the 1830s to present. He had no intention of telling this professor the truth about the legend, and thought the "author" story was a clever cover. To protect himself further, he created a fictitious e-mail account under the name of Timothy Benson.

He sent off the e-mail expecting it would be several weeks before he would get a response, if he got one at all. He asked Dr. Rutland to get back to him even if he couldn't help, so he could begin looking elsewhere.

Back at his maps, Joseph just stared, wondering just how far off he really was. He knew if you drew an 18° angle on a map, the closer you are to the point where the legs of the angle meet, the difference is minor. The cipher had told him the treasure was five miles from the two falls on the Raquette River, at a heading of 125°. The further away you are from where you take your heading, the further apart the legs of the angle become. That means, the further off course you are. "I could have been looking a mile or more off course," he decided. He was disappointed his limited Boy Scout training didn't give him the tools to figure out the exact change in compass headings from the 1830s, or to calculate the deviation five miles from the point where he takes the heading.

Frustrated and impatient, as a back-up plan, Joseph shot off an e-mail to the director of The Ranger School in Wanakena, only a seven mile drive from Cranberry Lake. The school is part of the State University of New York, College of Environmental Science and Forestry, and offers programs in surveying technology. "With their knowledge in surveying, someone at The Ranger School surely could help me," he thought. He used the same "treasure hunt author" story and fictitious name as a cover for his request.

NINE

JUDGE PENNINGTON stopped by the state police barracks on his way into court Wednesday morning. He wanted to meet Sergeant Perry personally and he wanted an update on the investigation. The news was not good.

Perry told the judge the investigation would ramp into high gear today. All state police in New York and surrounding states had already been notified to keep an eye out for the Land Rover. Judge Kelly's credit card and cell phone records were being reviewed as they spoke.

Pennington brought up the subject of the press again. In the interest of protecting Judge Kelly's wife, he had hoped he could convince the station commander to keep the story out of the media for as long as possible.

Sergeant Perry explained he was in a difficult position. "Judge, I understand and appreciate your concern for Mrs. Kelly, but a missing judge is a big deal. Anyway, the case is already listed on the blotter and that's a public document. Anybody can look at it. In fact, the press is in here every day to look at it. I would be crucified if I tried to remove it now. Certainly, we won't release any details of the investigation," he said. "Who knows where this is going to end up. If foul play is involved it will be a criminal case and then everything changes. I will make you this promise Judge, I'll keep you informed, best I can, of any major developments, and I'll give you a heads up before anything new is released."

"Fair enough." Pennington thanked the sergeant and headed the few hundred yards down the road to the court.

The mood in the Administrative Law Court was solemn when Judge Pennington arrived at nine thirty. He updated Val and Brendan on his meeting with the state police and then gave a little speech. "We all have to be strong and we need to give the state police anything they require. Judge Kelly would expect no less."

Kelly had been involved in well over a hundred cases over the past five years. It would take Val several hours to assemble the data investigators had requested. Brendan offered to help with the phones so she wouldn't be interrupted. Meanwhile, in Pennington's office, he updated the judge on Judge Kelly's current cases.

"He has only twenty-seven open cases in various stages," Brendan explained. "But, most are in the discovery stage. It would be months before any action would be required on these. There were also a few cases where minor motions required a ruling. But these cases could be put off for a month or two."

"Let's wait a few days before we reschedule any motion hearings," Pennington told Brendan. Pennington had developed considerable respect for the young clerk. Brendan had grown into the job quickly and had a good command of the current docket and the details of each of the cases.

He went on to tell Pennington, "Judge Kelly had scheduled a fishing vacation for the second week of April. So, there's really only one case that needs immediate attention."

"The Resort case." Pennington was more than a little familiar with the matter.

Brendan nodded, "Closing arguments are scheduled for next Monday. Judge Kelly was just making the final edits to his ruling. What do you think we should do?"

"Why don't you schedule a two p.m. conference call with the three parties? I want you on that call, and schedule a court reporter, too. I want this on the record."

"Consider it done. Anything else?"

"Can you get me a copy of Judge Kelly's notes and his draft ruling in the case?"

"Sure thing Judge. I've got everything on my desk." Brendan knew Judge Kelly's office was still off limits. He'd left a hard copy of the draft ruling on Kelly's desk, but the original was in his computer along with the judge's notes.

"Give me ten minutes to pull everything together."

While Brendan was gathering the information, Pennington called Judge Kelly's home.

"Kelly residence," the male voice said. "Bob, this is Noah Pennington." Pennington recognized the voice as Judge Kelly's son. He knew him since he was a child and had helped him get into law school. Bob Kelly, Jr., was following in his father's footsteps.

"When did you get in town?"

"I got here about an hour ago. Your wife just left. That was kind of her to stay over."

"How's your mom doing?"

"She's still pretty upset," Bob, Jr. said.

"That's to be expected, I am so glad you're able to be here for her."

Pennington told the younger Kelly about his visit with the state police commander.

"I know. He called a few minutes ago and told me you had been there. By the way, Sergeant Perry also told me that you had tried to keep this out of the press. Thanks for trying. My mom and I appreciate your efforts."

"I don't think I was too successful," Pennington said.

"We understand the position the state police are in. They have to keep the public informed, especially since Dad is such a public man."

Pennington took note of Bob Kelly's use of the present tense. That's good, he thought, that he is not referring to his father in the past tense.

"Is there anything I can do for you or your mom?"

"Not really," Bob Kelly said. "The state police are going to be back here in an hour or so for some more questions. We'll stay in touch."

"Let me know if there is anything you need."

He thanked Judge Pennington for his call.

Just as Pennington hung up the phone Brendan returned with two file folders containing Judge Kelly's notes in the Resort case as well as the draft final ruling.

"I should have written summaries of the other active cases for the state police in a couple of hours," he added.

Before he began gathering that information, Brendan set up the conference call Pennington had requested. LaCroix and McCalister each agreed immediately, asking what it was about. "You'll have to ask the judge at two p.m., I was just asked to make the arrangements." As Pennington had requested, he didn't mention that it was not Judge Kelly who had ordered the call.

At the APA, Ricky Hartman's secretary told Brendan that Mr. Hartman was out of the office but she would call him and let him know. "The judge expects him to be on the call," Brendan told her firmly. "He'll be there," she said. She promised to call back within the hour to confirm.

TEN

THE FAIRVIEW Motel, just four hundred yards up the road from the Ray Brook State Police barracks, was one of a dozen inexpensive motels along the highway between Saranac Lake and Lake Placid. It was just down the road from the Tail O' the Pup BBQ restaurant. The Fairview was one of several motels that had closed over the past two years because of the slow economy and the downturn in tourism.

The vehicle was behind the building and couldn't be seen from the road. Trooper Mike Schalit had discovered it during a routine patrol to make sure homeless people or drug dealers weren't using the vacant rooms. The late model black Land Rover contained clear and convincing evidence a crime had been committed.

When Anthony Goss arrived, Schalit had already cordoned off a large area with crime scene tape and was waiting in his cruiser. Goss was senior investigator at the Major Crimes Unit in Ray Brook.

The Land Rover was facing the back of the motel. Careful not to touch anything, Goss took a quick look around. He didn't open any of the doors to the vehicle, but he could see there was no body inside. However, there appeared to be a bullet hole in the upper corner of the driver's side windshield. On the inside of the windshield, and the side window, there were blood spatters along with what appeared to be tissue and bone fragments. Blood was on the passenger seat as well. It was not pretty. The forensics report would help make a final determination, but it looked like someone sitting in the driver's seat had been shot, possibly from the passenger seat or, more probably from the rear seat. Whoever had been in the driver's seat probably had not survived. He couldn't see a weapon through the windows.

Goss went over to talk to Schalit. "Where's forensics?"

"On their way sir. Should be here any minute."

"Did you run the plate?"

Schalit nodded. "It belongs to that missing judge."

Goss ordered Schalit to stay until forensics had completed their work. "Tell the guys I want that bullet found. It's either got to be in the wall of the building or on the ground between the vehicle and the building. Tell them to not to bother coming back unless they have it." He also ordered Schalit to move his car.

"I don't want anyone on the back side of this building. Since we can't be seen from the road, let's not advertise we're here. Turn your bar lights off. And, don't let anybody around that corner. When forensics are done here have them take the vehicle to the garage."

Goss was grateful the State Police had just built a new forensics garage at the Ray Brook barracks. Otherwise the vehicle would have had to be driven to Olean, at least three hundred and fifty miles away.

Back at the office, Goss asked Sergeant Perry to brief him on the information gathered since the missing persons report first came in. Perry gave him the written reports from the interviews with Mrs. Kelly, Judge Pennington and Brendan Martin. He told Goss, "Judge Kelly was involved in about a hundred cases over the past five years. He has twenty-seven open cases, most of them minor. The biggest is the Adirondack Mountain and Lake Resort case."

"I've been reading about that Resort case in the papers for years."

"It's been controversial. We'll have Judge Kelly's complete case list with contact information for the involved parties this afternoon. Forensics will go over Judge Kelly's office this afternoon as well. It was secured last night."

"Are the Resort offices in Tupper Lake?"

"As far as I know they are."

"I'll call Frank Johnson, the station commander in Tupper and have him assign one of his people to be our point man there. We'll start with the parties involved in this Resort case. I'm sure a lot is at stake there . . . for both sides."

Johnson told Goss, "The investigator who worked out of Tupper had just retired. But, I can give you my best sergeant, Jerry Doolin."

"Fine, have Doolin here in Ray Brook for a seven a.m. meeting."

Jerry was excited to get the assignment. Some time away from this desk will be a relief, he thought, not minding that Thursday and Friday were supposed to be his days off. Then he remembered his plans with Joseph. He'd have to reschedule their excursion to the transfer station.

It was four rings before the phone was answered. "Hey, Joe Joe. How are you this fine day?"

"First, it's Joseph not Joe Joe. Second, I have a headache, so it's not a fine day, third, why are you in such a good mood, and finally, why would my bald-headed friend be calling me in the middle of his work day?"

"I'm calling to let you know I won't be able to make it on Friday. A big case has come up. I'm going to be heading up the Tupper Lake part of the investigation."

"Well, that's disappointing. I wanted to talk to you about something. Any chance we could have dinner tonight?"

"Sure, buddy, why don't we meet at the lodge around seven. My turn to buy. There's something I wanted to talk to you about as well."

ELEVEN

"Good Morning."

"Morning?" Val looked up toward the voice. She was surprised to see a state trooper. She glanced at the clock. "Oh my, I guess eleven forty-five is still morning. I'm so sorry," she said, "we don't have all the information pulled together yet. You're early."

"I'm not here for that. I'm Sergeant Perry, the Station Commander from up the road. I'm here to see Judge Pennington if he's in. By the way, you can call me when you're done with those reports and I'll have one of our investigators stop in to pick them up." Perry handed her his card.

"That's a relief, we need the extra time."

"The forensics team will be here this afternoon as well."

"Okay, let me tell Judge Pennington you're here."

Pennington was surprised to hear who was in the reception area. He came out to greet his visitor.

"Good morning again, Judge. Could we speak privately?"

"Of course, let's go into my office."

The Sergeant closed the office door behind him and sat in one of the large leather chairs across the desk from the judge.

Val walked over to Brendan's desk and before she said a word, Brendan said, "I saw him, Why is he here?"

"Don't know. I wish I knew what they were talking about," Val said.

"We'll know soon enough. Remember, Val, patience is a virtue"

"Stop saying that."

"Look, we've got to get these reports done. Judge Pennington will let us know what's going on as soon as the trooper leaves."

"He's not a trooper, he's a sergeant. In fact, he's the station commander."

"So? Let's get back to work."

Inside Pennington's office, Perry started the conversation. "Judge, I'm a blunt man and I'll keep this short. We found Judge Kelly's car about two hours ago."

"And the judge . . . ?"

"No sign of him. Because it's a missing judge we're dealing with, I've turned the case over to our Bureau of Criminal Investigation. Their forensics people are going over the vehicle now. Look, I'm here because I promised I would keep you updated. The press is going to be all over this in a few hours. We're asking the Kelly family to not speak with the press. I'm asking you to do the same. It's your choice, but I sure hope you'll cooperate with us on this."

"Of course, we'll do anything you ask." Pennington's mind was beginning to race.

"I told your secretary our forensics people will be here this afternoon."

"That's fine." the judge said, "What else can we do to help?"

"A prayer would be good right now. And Judge, thanks for your help with the press. We'll be in touch. As I told you this morning I'll keep you updated as much as I can."

"Thanks for coming by personally, I appreciate it."

Pennington escorted the sergeant to the front door. "Thanks again," the judge said.

"You bet."

Without saying a word to Val or Brendan, Pennington went back to his office and closed the door. He had to think. Pennington knew Sergeant Perry was not telling him everything. Missing person cases, even cases about missing judges, aren't turned over the BCI unless there's evidence of a crime.

Val and Brendan had never seen the judge close his office door when no visitors were present. They said nothing to each other, but they could see the concern in each other's faces.

Val kept an eye on the lights on the phone and saw that Pennington made no calls. Maybe that's a good sign, she thought.

Only fifteen minutes had gone by when Pennington came out. He reached into his pocket and pulled out two twenty dollar bills, handed them to Brendan, and asked if he would take a run to the Chinese buffet place in Saranac Lake and get lunch for the three of them.

"When you get back, I'll update you both on what the Sergeant told me."

"Sure thing Judge."

It took only thirty minutes for Brendan to return. Lunch was set up on a table in the courtroom. They frequently had Chinese and the tradition was to eat family style. Brendan had gotten three entrée items from the menu and a large container of fried rice.

Over lunch Pennington told Brendan and Val the little he knew. "I've made some decisions," he said. "First, I'm going to take over the Resort case for now. We're going to reschedule the hearing for a week from Monday. That will give me enough time to go over the record. Brendan, keep your schedule open for next week. I'm going to need your help." He looked at Val. "Clear my schedule completely. Move any of my hearings you need to. Let's move them out at least thirty days. And, from now through next week, the only calls I'll take are my wife, anybody from the Kelly family, and the state police. Questions?"

There was a moment of awkward silence before Brendan spoke up. "What about Judge Kelly? He's been working on this case for ten years. He's got a lot invested in it."

Normally, Judge Pennington didn't like his decisions being questioned. However he respected Brendan for defending Kelly. He put his hand on the young man's shoulder, "Brendan, I admire your loyalty to Judge Kelly. If he's back in time, the case is his. If not, he would be the first to want to see the case come to a conclusion."

"You're right, Judge, I'm sorry."

"Nothing to be sorry about. Kelly would be proud of you." Pennington looked at the clock on the wall, "Now, we have a conference call in fifteen minutes."

Val cleaned up from lunch while Brendan started getting the parties on the line for the conference call.

At precisely two o'clock all was ready. Without revealing that Judge Kelly was not present, Brendan had instructed the court reporter to begin the recording as soon as the judge came on the line.

Pennington picked up his phone.

"Good afternoon everyone, I know you had very short notice for this conference, so I thank you for making yourselves available. No doubt you've already figured out I'm not Judge Kelly. For the record, my name is Judge Noah Pennington. I will be presiding over this call. Again, for the record, the participants in this call are Ms. Alicia LaCroix, attorney for the plaintiff. Are you here, Ms. LaCroix?"

"I'm here, Your Honor."

"Mr. Richard Hartman for the Adirondack Park Agency. Are you on the line Mr. Hartman?"

"I'm here, Judge."

"Thank you Mr. Hartman. For the defendant, Mr. Shane Baxter, Mr. Baxter?"

"Yes Judge."

"Also with us, as an observer, is our law clerk, Brendan Martin. Are you still here Brendan?"

"Yes Sir, Judge"

"Finally, our court reporter today is Kathy Johnson. Are you here Ms. Johnson?"

"Yes, Your Honor, I'm here."

"All present and accounted for. With the exception of Mr. Baxter, I know all of you. Ladies and gentlemen, I have some bad news. Judge Kelly has not been seen or heard from for almost forty eight hours. The state police were notified twenty-four hours ago and this morning, Judge Kelly's car was found. There was no sign of the judge. As of three hours ago, the case was turned over to the Bureau of Criminal Investigation. We're very concerned for Judge Kelly, but the business of this court will not come to a halt because of these events. Therefore, effective immediately, I will take over as presiding judge for this case. Monday's hearing will be postponed one week. I expect you to be prepared for that hearing. The rules will be the same, a one-hour summation for each side. Ms. LaCroix and Mr. Hartman, you can split your hour anyway you please. And, I don't want any surprises. Are there any questions?"

LaCroix spoke up first. "Judge, once we go off the record, I have a question about Judge Kelly."

"Anybody else have a question?"

"Yes, Judge, this is Shane Baxter. I want to inform the Court that we had planned to introduce some new evidence at Monday's hearing. It's not complicated evidence and shouldn't affect the court's ability to make a final ruling from the bench, if that's what you're planning."

LaCroix jumped in, "We object, Your Honor. We weren't made aware of any new evidence."

Baxter, expecting this response remained calm, "This evidence just came to our attention yesterday, Your Honor. We planned on notifying the court and the plaintiffs tomorrow."

"Alright, here's what we'll do. Mr. Baxter, I want a motion requesting permission to introduce this new evidence on my desk by Monday. And, it better be good. Plaintiffs will have until Friday to respond. Be prepared to argue the motion before final arguments in a week and a half. Each side will have fifteen minutes. Again, Ms. LaCroix and Mr. Hartman, you can split your fifteen minutes any way you like. Is there anything else?"

After a short pause, Judge Pennington spoke up again,

"Fine, I have two more items before we finish. First, the state police have asked this office to not make any statements to the press. I agreed. At this point, I'm not inclined to issue a gag order, but I'm going to ask each of you to not talk to the press during the investigation. Make no mistake, if I see even one word, on or off the record, from anybody associated with this case, I'll issue a gag order immediately. You all had better let everyone in your office know the rules as well. Does anybody have a problem with that?"

Everyone agreed.

"Finally, I have cleared my schedule for the next week to review the record in this case. I won't be taking any calls during this time. If it's an emergency, contact Brendan. He'll pass on anything important. That's all I have. If nobody else has anything to add to the record, then we're done. Ms. LaCroix, you had a question off the record?"

Everyone stayed on the line to hear the question.

"Yes, Judge. I don't think the state police would have turned a missing person's case over to their Bureau of Criminal Investigation unless there was evidence of foul play. Did they tell you what they found?"

"Ms. LaCroix, the state police have a job to do, and it's not to keep us informed of details of their investigation. I am not going to speculate on what they may, or may not, have found. And, I suggest, Ms. LaCroix, you avoid speculation as well. Let's let the state police do their job."

"Thank you everybody, I'll see you in a week and a half"

TWELVE

THE FIRST call came into the Administrative Law Office at 3:25 p.m. The Saranac newspaper wanted a comment regarding Judge Kelly's disappearance. Judge Pennington had written a simple statement that Brendan was instructed to read or fax to the press:

> *All of us in the Administrative Law Court are concerned about the whereabouts of Judge Kelly. Our thoughts today are with Judge Kelly, Mrs. Kelly and the Kelly family.*
>
> *This office will not make any further statements during the investigation. We have complete confidence in the New York State Police, and we are going to let them do their job.*

The reporter then asked Brendan, "Can you give me a little background on Judge Kelly?"

"I gave you the only statement we have."

"How long was Judge Kelly with the Administrative Court?"

"No comment."

"Did the state police have any leads in the case?"

"No comment."

"How old was Judge Kelly?"

Brendan didn't like the use of the past tense in the reporter's questions and said again, "No comment."

"What's going to happen to the Adirondack Mountain and Lake Resort case?"

"Look, I gave you the only statement this office is going to release. We will have nothing else to say to the media as long as the investigation is ongoing. Thank you for your call."

Brendan hung up and let Pennington know that the media circus had started. While he was in Pennington's office, more calls came in.

Brendan stayed until eight p.m. answering media calls. He was surprised that *The New York Times*, the Associated Press, even CNN and FOX News were calling. The cable news people wanted to know if there was a staging area for the media. They said they might be sending reporters and satellite trucks to the area.

Before he left the office, Brendan printed Judge Pennington's statement on court letterhead and made copies, just in case he needed them for tomorrow.

§

The Cranberry Lake Lodge has been an institution in the western part of the Adirondacks for more than one hundred years. Located on the north shore of the lake, the lodge was the only place you can get dinner in Cranberry Lake this time of year.

Jerry was surprised to see Joseph come in with an old, worn leather briefcase. Joseph worked from home and never carried a briefcase in public.

"Hey Joe," Jerry said with a smile.

"The name is Joseph. When are you going to get that through that chrome dome of yours?"

"I have a short-term memory problem when it comes to your name. Maybe if you bought a rug for that bald head of yours, stuff wouldn't leak out."

"I'll take that under advisement. So, what's the briefcase about? If you're going to try to sell me something, I'm leaving."

Jerry had arrived before Joseph and had taken a table by the fireplace in the dining room. Now, even though there was nobody else in the room, Joseph asked if they could move to a corner table by the windows, overlooking the lake. "There's a little more privacy over there," Joseph said.

These two men had been best of friends for a long time, and other than the friendly banter over Joseph's name and Jerry's bald head, they seldom engaged in small talk. As soon as they were settled at their new table with drinks, Jerry asked, "So, what's up, buddy?"

Joseph undid the straps on the briefcase, pulled out the bible and set it on the table.

"That looks old," Jerry said.

"It is. About two-hundred years old. It's my family bible and it once belonged to Joseph Bonaparte."

"This isn't about the treasure is it?"

"Jerry, there is something about the treasure I've never told you. Look inside the front cover."

Jerry could tell that his friend was excited. He opened the bible and saw four hand-written lines and a signature.

"I don't read French," he said. "What does it say?"

"First of all, that's Joseph Bonaparte's signature at the bottom. He wrote the four lines. Here's the translation." Joseph reached back into the briefcase, pulled out a single piece of paper, and handed it to Jerry. On the top of the page was the four-line translation. On the bottom of the page was the deciphered message from the medallion.

Jerry read the translation. "I don't understand. What does it mean?"

"Look inside the back cover."

Jerry turned to the back cover and looked. "I still don't understand."

"Look at the third line again. *The medallion is your guide.*"

"So, what does it mean?"

"That's the medallion inside the back cover."

Jerry turned to the back of the bible again and was studying the medallion when Joseph repeated, "*The medallion is your guide.* The map to your freedom . . . the map to the Spanish Royal Treasure you idiot"

"You don't really believe all this do you? There's no map here."

"Look buddy, I've spent thirty years trying to figure this out. I never told you about the bible because I knew you thought this whole thing was silly. Deep down, even you thought I was a little crazy."

"Just a little," Jerry said. "After all, you did ruin a marriage over this stuff."

Joseph repeated again, "The medallion stupid, *Dumas is your key.*"

"What does that mean?"

"Have you ever heard of the Dumas cipher?"

"Actually, I have. It was used by the founding fathers during the Revolutionary war to keep sensitive war plans out of British hands."

"Look at the markings on the medallion. I found the Dumas cipher code on the internet and used it to translate the markings."

Jerry was staring at the medallion and Joseph could see that Jerry was thinking. What he was thinking, Joseph wasn't sure.

"The bottom of that white sheet is the Dumas translation."

"You're kidding!" Jerry was staring at the Dumas translation.

Snowshoe River | 2 falls | 125° | 5 miles.

"Okay. Explain."

Joseph's excitement about finally sharing this with someone was almost uncontainable. "Come on, stay with me buddy. That's where the treasure is. Snowshoe River, by the two falls. Find the heading of 125° and go five miles."

"I've never heard of a Snowshoe River."

"Neither had I, but I figured it out three years ago."

Jerry was stunned. "You knew all this three years ago and never told me."

"I knew what you thought of the treasure and I wanted to find it, to prove you wrong."

"Don't tell me you found it?"

"No. But I've been looking. You're not going to believe this, but just yesterday I figured out why I haven't found it."

"Really?"

"Yeah, asshole, really! Did you know that magnetic north shifts every year and compass headings from the 1830s are very different than today?"

"I've never really thought about it. Wasn't there something on the news about that?"

"That's right." Joseph was getting even more excited. "It was on the news just yesterday. That's when I figured it out. I've been looking in the wrong place because I've been using a compass heading from 1830.

"First of all, where the hell is Snowshoe River?"

Joseph couldn't stop smiling. "Think buddy, think."

"Come on, you've been thinking about this for thirty years. I haven't known about it for thirty minutes. Where is it?"

"How do you say 'snowshoe' in French?"

"I don't know. How?

"Raquette, it's the Raquette River."

Jerry couldn't believe what he was hearing. "No shit." Even he was getting excited now. "Did you find the two falls?"

"There was only one trail between Lake Bonaparte and the Raquette River in 1830. It's about where Route 3 is today." He paused to let Jerry comprehend what he had just said. "Remember, there were no dams on the river in 1830," he reminded Jerry.

It didn't take Jerry long. "Piercefield Falls and Setting Pole Falls?"

Joseph was leaning forward, pleased that his friend was finally getting into it.

"That's right. Now imagine a compass heading of about 125° and about five miles away. You can't miss it. You can see it from the road. It's unmistakable!"

Jerry sat silent for a moment thinking about the view from Route 3 near the current dams. "Not Big Tupper?"

Joseph couldn't stand it any longer. Both fists pounded the table.

"Yes . . . Big Tupper!"

"I can't believe it."

"Believe it my bald-headed friend, believe it."

Joseph took a deep breath. He needed to calm down. Both men just sat there, not saying a word for almost a full minute. Jerry had to absorb everything he had just heard. Joseph wanted his best friend to fully grasp what this all meant.

Finally, Jerry spoke up. "So, what do you do now?"

"I go find the treasure, idiot. But first, I need to find out how far off course I have been."

"And how do you propose to do that?"

"I've got my ways."

"Why are you telling me all this now?"

"Because you're my best friend. Because I'm excited. Because I couldn't keep it to myself anymore. You're the only person I can share this with."

"Joseph, I'm happy for you. This is remarkable. But, I'm having a hard time getting my head around all this. I just can't believe it. Do you *really* think it's there?"

"I *know* it's there." Joseph paused for a moment. "Will you help me?"

"You know I will. But how?"

"I bought two new metal detectors and one of them requires two people to operate. It's a beauty. You'll love it. Maybe on one of your days off we could walk the property."

"That would be fun. What do you think the treasure might be worth?" Jerry had never asked this question before because he didn't want to encourage his friend with some wild goose chase.

"If what's been passed down through the family is true, and so far it has been, it could be upwards of $500 million."

Jerry just sat there in stunned silence.

"I still can't believe it."

"Can't believe what sweetie?" Ashley, their waitress, appeared out of nowhere and was already putting a fresh round of drinks on the table.

Jerry looked up at Ashley, "I can't believe you knew I was ready for another diet cola."

Joseph chimed in, "and, I can't believe you knew we're ready to order . . . sweetie."

"I'm just psychic like that."

Neither of the men needed to look at the menu. Both ordered open steak sandwiches, medium-well, and a baked potato. Jerry asked for Italian dressing and Joseph asked for Blue Cheese.

As soon as Ashley was gone, Joseph said, "There is nobody in my life I would rather share this with then you, my shiny headed friend."

"Joey, how did you keep this search up for thirty years? Didn't you ever feel like giving up?"

"Five hundred million dollars provides a lot of motivation. Anyway, let's change the subject. You said on the phone you wanted to talk to me about something."

"We'll talk about it another time. This news is too good to change the subject."

Jerry had planned on talking to Joseph about his drinking. He was worried about him and was going to offer to take him to an AA meeting in Star Lake some Friday night. It was going to be a difficult conversation and he just couldn't bring it up now. He had not seen Joseph this happy for years. He was genuinely pleased for his friend.

"You mentioned earlier the news story about magnetic north shifting. Does that mean the 125° heading is wrong?"

"Yes, but I'm not sure how far off it is. You're going to love this. I used a phony name and e-mail address and contacted a couple of college professors yesterday asking for their help. I didn't tell them about the treasure, I told them I was an author writing a book. One was chairman of the Geology Department at RPI. The other was the director of The Ranger School in Wanakena. I'm waiting for their answers."

"You think they'll get back to you?"

"I guess we'll find out." Joseph was ready to change the subject. "So, tell me about this big new case of yours."

"I can't." There was a pause. "Not because I can't. Because, I don't know. Apparently there's a big case in Saranac Lake and somehow it has ties to Tupper. I have no idea what it's about, but I'll find out tomorrow. We have a big meeting with the BCI in Ray Brook at seven a.m."

The two men finished their meals, said their goodbye's, and were headed out of the lodge by nine thirty. In the parking lot Jerry gave Joseph a big hug and said, "I'm happy for you buddy. And I'm sorry I didn't believe you all these years."

They went their separate ways.

THIRTEEN

DRIVING TO the meeting in Ray Brook, Jerry couldn't stop thinking about the remarkable news he had heard the night before. He wondered if he was being sucked into Joseph's fantasy. He went over everything Joseph had told him the night before and concluded there may actually be something to the legend. It was four thirty a.m. when he crossed the Raquette River in Piercefield on Route 3. Even though it was still dark, he looked to the south. In his mind's eye he could see the ski trails about five miles away at the Big Tupper Ski area, which was built on the side of Mt. Morris, just a few miles south of the Village of Tupper Lake. He had seen this scene for real thousands of times.

He needed to stop in the Tupper Lake barracks to change into his uniform. The barracks were almost directly across State Route 30 from the entrance to the ski area. As he pulled into the parking lot, Jerry remembered that a huge resort was being planned around Big Tupper. In fact, he remembered seeing something in the papers about an important hearing regarding permits that was taking place soon. He couldn't remember the details.

After a quick change into his uniform, and a few minutes at his desk, Jerry headed out for the forty-five minute drive to Ray Brook. An eighties classic rock CD was playing, but at six a.m. he switched to North Country Public Radio to get a weather report. The headline on the news was about a missing judge who worked in Ray Brook. Jerry turned up the radio:

73

. . . Judge Kelly had been hearing the controversial Adirondack Mountain and Lake Resort case planned for the property of the Big Tupper Ski Area in Tupper Lake. Final arguments are scheduled for Monday. There has been no word yet from the court if the hearing is going to be rescheduled. Other than expressing their concern for Judge Kelly and the Kelly family, and their confidence in the State Police, the Court said they would have no further comment on the case.

Now I know what I'll be doing for the next few days, Jerry thought.

As he drove by the administrative court building, he saw a satellite truck turning into their parking lot. Beyond it, he saw three more trucks already parked, with their satellite dishes extended toward the sky. Even from the road, he could see the see the reporters awash in artificial lights holding their microphones as they did their live stand-ups. On one truck, he could see the distinctive letters of CNN.

They're going to need someone down here to play traffic cop soon, he thought. Just a few hundred more yards up the road, he turned into the parking area for the Ray Brook barracks of the state police.

He was fifteen minutes early and everybody was already there except the senior investigator. State police training taught these men and women to never be late. In fact, "Lombardi Time" was the rule every trooper lived by. The legendary coach of the Green Bay Packers, Vince Lombardi, always taught his men to be fifteen minutes early. Every organization with a reputation for efficiency and organization operated on "Lombardi Time."

"Tony Goss walked in and said, "it's 6:55, everybody's here, let's get started."

Jerry had worked with everyone at the table at one time or another over the past twenty-two years. To Goss's right was Investigator Thomas Cook, another BCI man. Next to him was Sergeant Sam Perry from the Ray Brook barracks. To Goss's left sat Shelia Kenyon from forensics and Edward Reynolds, the Essex County District Attorney. Jerry sat at the other end of the table, across from Goss. In a chair against the wall behind Jerry was the State Police public information officer.

"We've got a big one on our hands people," Goss started. You saw the media gathering down the road. I've asked the district attorney to be in on this from the start."

Goss asked Perry to summarize the investigation to date. He gave a brief overview of the several interviews with Mrs. Kelly, Judge Pennington and the law clerk. He also summarized the interviews with the convenience store clerks. He finished with how Judge Kelly's vehicle was found.

"Thanks Sam." Goss then turned the floor over to Shelia, a feisty woman who never gave up looking for clues. She wore her short black hair in a pageboy cut. "Shelia's people have worked all night so we would have as much information as possible this morning," Goss added.

"As you heard, the vehicle was found behind the Fairview Motel just up the road. There was clear evidence of violence. Blood, tissue and bone fragments were on the inside front windshield, dashboard and side window. There was a bullet hole through the windshield. A nine millimeter slug was found in a door of the motel. Blood type matches Judge Kelly's. We took hair samples from his home so we should have DNA results in a few days. That will confirm if it's the judge's blood and tissue. There was a great deal of blood in the passenger seat and on the floor on the passenger side of the car. It appeared the body may have been moved from the driver's seat to the passenger seat.

"We did find a few strands of hair in the back seat that did not belong to Judge Kelly. Those are being analyzed now. Fingerprints appear to be Kelly's. We got matches when we went over his office yesterday afternoon. There was no evidence of any struggle at the office. Employees tell us that nothing appears to have been out of place when they arrived Tuesday morning. They are doing an inventory to see if anything is missing. As you know, it's hard to tell sometimes if papers have been taken.

"Finally, Tony, it's a gravel parking lot, and it appears the vehicle drove in, parked, then left and returned again. We've collected gravel samples from the tires. With some luck we'll be able to match it to a specific area after the body turns up. We still are going over the interior of the vehicle and may have more, but that's all we have so far."

"Good work Shelia. And tell your people thanks for working all night. I've asked Tom to work associations and motivation. Tom?"

Tom Cook was a fifty-year-old career cop who had been with the BCI for twenty years. His sandy hair hid his age well.

"Thanks Tony. Nothing significant yet. No enemies, no arguments, no apparent problems with family or work associates. Seems the judge was the perfect family man and upstanding citizen. Everybody Sam's people talked with insisted there was absolutely no way he was having an affair. That said, the hairs found in the back seat appear to be from a female. Shelia's people are still analyzing them, but we know they don't match the wife. If they aren't from a female then they're from a male with long blond hair. We've got some more digging to do here. I'm checking *la femme*, as they say. Maybe it was a one night stand or a moment of weakness. There's always a first time.

"Moving on, the judge has a number of active cases, and one appears to be controversial. That's the Adirondack Mountain and Lake Resort case. It's been a bitter battle for ten years and a decision was supposed to be announced next Monday. Over the past five years he was involved with almost a hundred cases. I'm not really sure what's there yet, but the Resort case is the obvious starting point. Jerry, you'll be our Tupper Lake point man. Talk to everybody at the Resort offices and see what you come up with."

"Yes sir."

"I'll be talking with the APA people and this Adirondack Environmental Watch group. That's all I have for now."

"Thanks Tommy." Tony Goss paused and looked around the room. "We don't have a body people and that limits the investigation. We've driven the road between the judge's office and home several times, but since the vehicle was found at the Fairview, it looks like he may have never left Ray Brook, at least not alive. Sam Perry has a group assembled to search a wide area around the motel later this morning. Since there are no other clues at this point, I'm not sure in which haystack we begin looking for a body. We need more. I'm counting on you to get it."

"Now, the media. At this point, nothing is being released to them. The people at the court aren't talking to them either. At some point we may start holding daily briefings for them, we'll decide on that later this morning."

"Folks, we're still in that important window of opportunity. Whoever did this made a mistake somewhere. We just have to find it. If we don't get this solved quickly, we're not only going to have the media all over us, but public opinion will start turning against us. We're going to meet here at four p.m. every day for a wrap-up. Doolin, if you can't be here in person, I want you here by phone."

"One way or another, I'll be here."

"Let's get this one solved quickly people. Tommy said the Resort case is the obvious place to start. He's right, but remember, the truth is seldom obvious. If you get anything at all, I want to hear about it. Thanks everybody, see you at four."

Tommy Cook handed Jerry a file on the Resort case. Inside was a short briefing paper along with newspaper articles and printouts from the Adirondack Mountain and Lake Resort website. He had two contact names, Steve Cannon, the original Project Manager, and Shane Baxter, attorney.

Walking out of the building, Jerry saw the Saranac Lake newspaper sitting on a desk. The headline went across the entire top of the page.

RESORT CASE JUDGE MISSING
NEXT WEEK'S DECISION IN QUESTION

A photograph of Judge Kelly took up half the page, above the fold.

Driving back to Tupper Lake, Jerry thought about how he would approach the Resort people. When there is no suspect, everybody is suspect. He had been involved in thousands of investigations in his twenty-two years. The difference here was a very high-profile victim, which meant a great deal of scrutiny. Doolin couldn't recall a case where the district attorney had been brought in at the beginning of an investigation. Usually you never saw them until evidence began to point to a specific suspect.

The message was clear, this was no usual case.

FOURTEEN

SHANE WALKED into Maureen's office with a new sense of purpose and his copy of *The Art of War* in his hand. "I can see why this is read by so many business people. It's a masterpiece on strategy. I'd never thought about how military strategy and business strategy were so closely aligned." At her suggestion, Shane had taken part of the previous day off to read the book. "By the way," he said. "It's given me some new ideas on how I'm going to change my final summation."

"Good, I look forward to reading it." Maureen was pleased the book had helped but had really called him into her office this morning to discuss how Judge Pennington taking over the case would affect them.

"I'm not really sure," he said. "The parties in the case had a conference call with the judge. He's planning on going over the record during the next week. He's got a lot of reading to do in a week. I mentioned on the call we had new evidence, and Ms. Bitch started to raise holy hell. We'll have a short motions hearing regarding the new evidence just before final arguments. The judge has given us each fifteen minutes."

"Do you think he'll grant the motion?" Maureen asked.

"I think so. I'm not so sure about getting a final ruling though. I was pretty sure Judge Kelly was going to give us a decision from the bench, but I don't know about Judge Pennington."

There was a tap on the door and Tommy poked his head in, "Maureen, there is a state trooper here to see you." Tommy then lowered his voice,

"He asked for Mr. Cannon, but I told him he was no longer with us and that you had taken over as project manager."

"Show him in, Tommy. Shane, why don't you stay? Let's see what this is about."

Tommy returned with Jerry Doolin and made the introductions, "Sergeant Doolin, this is Mrs. McCalister, our new project manager"

"Call me Maureen, please." They shook hands and Doolin was surprised at the firm handshake coming from this woman.

Shane didn't wait for Tommy to introduce them. He put his hand out, "I'm Shane Baxter. I'm the attorney for the Resort. How can we help you?"

Jerry shook his hand with a smile. "Oh, Mr. Baxter, I'm glad you're here, I wanted to see you too."

"Great, this will save you some time. You've got us both here."

"Actually," Jerry said, "I was hoping to speak to each of you privately. I hope that's not a problem."

"That is a problem," Shane started to say, but was interrupted by Maureen.

"That's no problem at all, Sergeant. Don't mind Shane . . . he's a lawyer. He's just doing his job." She turned to Shane. "I'll talk with the Sergeant and when we're finished, I'll bring him down to your office."

"Before I leave, can I ask what this is all about?"

"I'm sure you've heard about Judge Kelly's disappearance. The Resort is a major player in his biggest case." Jerry smiled. "Don't worry, nobody here is a suspect. I'm just getting some background information."

"Of course," Shane said. Although he knew nothing about criminal law, he was sure that everyone was probably a suspect. He decided not to push the issue.

"I'll be in my office."

"I'll be down shortly," Jerry said. "I don't expect this to take but a few minutes."

Maureen invited the Sergeant to sit at the round table in the back of her office. She never liked talking with people from behind her desk. It created too much of a barrier and prevented open discussion.

The conversation between Maureen and Jerry took more than an hour. To Maureen, the questions appeared to be routine. Jerry had a skill of making very pointed questions appear innocuous.

When she told Jerry about her drive to Tupper Lake Monday night, Maureen mentioned that she'd had dinner with a friend in Albany.

Jerry probed a little more. "Really? Every now and then I'm asked to teach at the State Police Academy, so I end up having to spend a fair amount of time in Albany myself. I don't like Albany much. Too many politicians . . . and I don't like politicians. By the way, do you know where the word "politics" comes from?"

Maureen thought for a moment, "I don't know, maybe Latin or something."

"Actually," Jerry said smiling, "it has a Greek derivation . . . 'Poly,' meaning many, and 'Ticks,' blood-sucking parasites."

They both laughed. Jerry asked where Maureen had dinner.

"I think the name of the place was Molly Malloy's. It was an Irish pub."

"Best fish and chips in Albany. I've eaten there lots of times."

"That's exactly what I had." Maureen told him. "It was good."

"Too bad you were there on a Monday. On Fridays and Saturdays they have a great band that plays traditional Irish music. And, as you probably figured out from my name, I do have a little Irish blood in these veins." Remembering the date, he said, "Wow, you just missed being there on St. Patrick's Day. I was there on St. Patrick's Day three years ago. The place was wild. What time did you get out of there?"

"I think it was just after eight. I didn't get to Tupper Lake until eleven thirty or so."

Getting back on track, Jerry asked how much she knew about the other major players in the Resort case.

"I really don't know anything about Ricky Hartman at the APA. I never met him, in fact. I did have lunch with Alicia LaCroix on Tuesday, just to introduce myself and get to know her a little."

"Know your enemy," Jerry said.

She was surprised. "You're familiar with Sun Tzu?"

"A great military strategist. Not bad stuff to know in my business."

"It's not bad stuff to know in any business."

"What were your impressions of Ms. LaCroix?"

"She's a very competent woman. She comes off as a sweet, concerned, environmentalist. But she can be tough as nails, ruthless, in fact."

"What makes you say that?"

"Sergeant, I spent a lot of years in the environmental movement before I finally saw the hypocrisy. Particularly with radical environmentalists like Alicia. And make no mistake about it, Alicia LaCroix is radical."

Jerry let the statement hang there, hoping Maureen would keep talking.

"I actually had a friend of mine who knows Alicia quite well put together a dossier on her. I wanted to know who I'd be dealing with."

Jerry smiled again. "Know your enemy. Smart."

"Well, I always prefer to know how cold the water is before I jump in."

"Sun Tzu would be proud of you. Any chance you could share that dossier with me?"

"I have no problem sharing it, as long as you keep it confidential. I would prefer Alicia not know I did this. And, I'm going to remove the name of the person who wrote it."

"That's fine," Jerry said. "Maureen, I've taken up way too much of your time. You have been very generous, thank you . . . and welcome to Tupper Lake."

"Thank you, Sergeant. I'm afraid Shane is probably having a cow by now. Lawyers are like that. Don't worry about him though, he's harmless."

On his way out of the office, Jerry stopped to look at the model of the development. "This is impressive. Off the record, I hope you get your permits, Tupper Lake needs a project like this."

"Thank you." As she was walking Jerry down the hall to Shane's office, they stopped at the copy machine and Maureen ran a copy of the seven-page dossier.

Jerry slipped the copy into the folder that was given to him at the Ray Brook briefing earlier. "Thanks again, Maureen. If I need anything else, I'll call."

As they reached Baxter's office, Maureen said, loud enough for Shane to hear, "No problem Sergeant, and don't worry about Shane there, a lot of bark, but no bite."

She winked at Shane and left.

Jerry knew before it began that the interview with this lawyer would not be as smooth as the one he'd just finished. His questions were basically the same, but Baxter limited himself to as few words as possible and never provided more information than was asked. Jerry had interviewed lawyers before and expected this.

He did offer one bit of new information. "This business with the missing judge is going to cost the Resort a lot of money."

Jerry just sat there, not saying a word, appearing to contemplate what Baxter had just said.

"This is just one more delay, in what has been a long series of delays. My people in New York are beginning to lose their patience. Every delay costs us money."

"How many investors are there in the project?"

"I'm not really sure. That's all handled out of corporate in New York City. My specialty is permitting issues, environmental studies, that kind of stuff."

"Are most of the investors from this area?" Jerry asked.

"Probably not. Again, I really don't know. There may be a couple. The company has never done a project in the Adirondacks before, and none of the partners are from here. That's not to say there are no investors from this area. Past projects this group has been involved with have been in Colorado, Texas and the Georgia coast."

Jerry hoped Baxter would offer a list of investors, but wasn't surprised when he didn't.

"I'd like to get a list of the money people if I could."

Shane knew he didn't have much of a choice in the matter. They could get it eventually.

"I'll call corporate and get a copy for you. Would you prefer me to fax it to you or e-mail?"

"Either way is fine. Here's my card. When do you think you could have it?"

"I should be able to get it to you by tomorrow." Shane didn't want to make it too easy for this trooper, but he didn't want it to appear he was stalling either.

"Thanks," Jerry said. "If there is any chance you could get it sooner, I'd really appreciate it."

The two men shook hands.

On his way out, Jerry poked his head in Maureen's open door and thanked her again.

"Shane didn't bite you did he?"

Jerry laughed, "No. In fact he was very helpful."

FIFTEEN

IT WAS three in the afternoon when Joseph checked his fictitious Timothy Benson e-mail account and saw he had a couple of new e-mails waiting.

"That was quick," he murmured.

He opened the e-mail from the chairman of the geology department at RPI.

Dear Timothy,

I am delighted to receive your e-mail. It's not every day I get such a request and I found it quite intriguing.

The information you seek is actually quite easy to find on the internet. If you go to the NOAA site:

http://www.ngdc.noaa.gov/geomagmodels/struts/historicPoint

You will find a historical magnetic declination calculator that will calculate the declination for any location for any sequence of years. I don't know exactly where your protagonist resides, so I just put in the Troy, New York, zip code (12180). The table is below. It seems the declination has changed by a bit over 7° since 1830 (note that the magnitude of change depends on where you are and the time interval).

What might be useful to calculate is how far off a treasure seeker would be if he/she had the wrong compass declination. It's simple trigonometry and can be calculated as 2 x [distance walked x sin(compass error/2)] and the direction you would have to walk to get to the right spot could also be calculated if you know what the original compass heading is. I could show you this with a simple drawing if you are interested. Say you were off in your compass orientation by 7°, then for every mile you traveled you would be off by 0.122 miles (645 feet).

Let me know if this helps. I would be happy to talk more with you about it.

Sincerely, Nathanael Rutland, PhD

Before he even finished reading the e-mail, Joseph clicked on the link to the NOAA website. He entered the zip code for Tupper Lake and the appropriate years. A chart appeared showing the shift for every year between 1830 and present. The declination in 1830 was 6°43' W. For 2012, it was 13°57' W. The difference was 7°14'.

"That still doesn't tell me how far off course I am. He looked at the e-mail again. "*It's simple trigonometry.*" "Simple for you," he muttered. Joseph was pleased he at least had a formula. He could find someone who could figure it out.

Joseph had never taken trigonometry in high school. He thought of a sharp high school student named Jonah who lived on Pennsylvania Avenue in Cranberry Lake. He couldn't remember his last name. He figured he could ask somebody at the diner in the morning.

Based on the sample calculation Professor Rutland provided for the declination difference in Troy, New York, Joseph figured he was off about .610 miles . . . just a little over half a mile.

I need to be exact, he thought.

The second e-mail was from the director of The Ranger School at

Wanakena. They taught surveying at The Ranger School, and maybe he could hire a few students to pinpoint the exact location. He was getting excited.

Timothy,

Thanks for the note. Interesting book you're working on. Treasure hunt books are always fun.

I am a licensed land surveyor (and professor and director) and would be pleased to provide you with some information regarding magnetic declinations. I will have to do a little work to find the declination from the 1830s for this area.

There is some more detailed information I will need. Specifically, in what geographic area will the character in your book be looking (I need a zip code), and second, how far away is it from where your character takes his/her compass heading to the actual location? This will allow me to calculate how far off course your character really is.

I look forward to working with you on this. It should be a fun project. Give me a call when you have a chance. I would like to discuss this with you further.

Chris

Joseph was pleased with himself that his "author" ruse worked so well. He sent a quick e-mail to both professors thanking them for their help and letting them know he would be in touch with them shortly.

He looked at the clock. It was almost four, "Time to celebrate." Joseph went to the kitchen to pour a drink. There wasn't enough vodka in the bottle on the counter so he pulled out a fresh bottle from the box in the cabinet. Sometime in the past two years he'd started to buy his vodka by the case. He filled a large tumbler with vodka and a little tonic and glanced at the newspapers he'd left on the counter.

While he used the "time to celebrate" line as an excuse, Joseph needed the drink. Even worse, once he started, he couldn't stop. It was not that he wouldn't stop, he couldn't stop.

Earlier in the day he'd seen the headlines in the *Watertown Daily Times* about the missing judge. In the back of his mind, he'd been wondering what effect that would have on the Resort case. He still wasn't sure whether a delay or a victory in the case would benefit his quest.

One way to get some answers was to call his lady friend. Alicia LaCroix wasn't in her office. The receptionist knew Joseph and told him she wasn't feeling well and had taken the day off. He called her at home.

"Alicia, how are you feeling?"

"I'm not really sure. It's been a rough day. I actually feel fine. I guess I'm just upset about the Judge Kelly news and my case being postponed."

"I saw the news in the papers. That's tough. I thought I would check in and see how you're doing. What's going to happen with that case?"

"I guess I'm disappointed we're not going to get a decision next week. We already have a new Judge and he's postponed the hearing for another week."

Joseph sensed a lack of something in her voice. He wasn't sure what it was, but decided to try and cheer her up. He also wanted more information.

"Since you no longer have the pressure of Monday's hearing, why don't you come up to Cranberry Lake? We'll have dinner at the lodge, and you can spend the night. We'll have some fun."

"You know Joseph, that's a good idea. I need to get away from here anyway. I might even take the day off tomorrow and just hang out with you for the day, if that's all right?"

"Sounds great! See you at seven?"

Joseph poured another drink and decided he needed to tidy up a bit before Alicia arrived. He looked at the clock. He had two hours.

SIXTEEN

PRECISELY AT four, Senior Investigator Tony Goss started the meeting of what he was now calling the "Kelly Task Force." Jerry was on speaker phone. Also attending the meeting by phone was Ed Reynolds, the district attorney in Elizabethtown. Reynolds was just listening at this point. When it came time to prosecute, he wanted to make sure there were no mistakes in the investigation that would affect his case.

"Okay everybody let me get a few things out of the way. We've decided to take advantage of the media down the street at the Administrative Court," Goss announced. "We held a press briefing at ten this morning. We didn't give any details, but we did release an 800 number for leads. The number has been broadcast on radio newscasts since noon. So far we've only had a few calls. Nothing significant to report. I suspect we'll start getting more after the TV news runs it at six and eleven tonight. It'll also be in the papers tomorrow. We will be giving the press an update every day at ten a.m. If events dictate, we'll update them more frequently. As an aside, the administrative court issued a short statement today saying their senior judge would be taking over that big Resort case Judge Kelly was handling. The final hearing scheduled for next Monday has been postponed one week. The court has been very cooperative. Everyone there has been interviewed and is listed as "source."

The BCI had a simple three tier system to prioritize the people they were investigating. Anybody being investigated as the case began was considered a "person of interest." As the investigation continued and interviews took place, people were upgraded to "suspect" or downgraded to "source." If there was more than one "suspect," they were prioritized with a simple letter system.

"Tommy, what do you have?"

"I met with Richard Hartman. He's the director of the APA. There is nothing there and he was able to account for his whereabouts Monday night. He's a source. Alicia LaCroix who is executive director of Adirondack Environmental Watch was out sick today. I'll talk to her tomorrow. Jerry in Tupper Lake did send over an interesting dossier on Ms. LaCroix. It was put together by the people at the Resort."

"Apparently corporate intelligence is alive and well," Goss interjected.

"Sure is. It actually was quite thorough too," Cook continued. "Ms. LaCroix had a run-in with the law about ten years ago in Oregon. The organization she was running in Oregon was involved in tree spiking and several people were severely injured. Apparently she's quite a radical environmentalist. It looks like they were trying to stop a development. Two activists affiliated with the organization were convicted. Ms. LaCroix wasn't accused of the spiking, just conspiracy. She was acquitted. Until I have a chance to talk to her, she's still listed as person of interest. Finally, I've been going over the cases the administrative court sent over. At first glance, nothing remarkable there, but there are a lot of cases. I'm still working it. That's all I have."

"Thanks Tommy. Let's get some more information on that Oregon thing. Run a background, then call the Oregon State Police and see if you can talk to somebody who was involved in that investigation ten years ago. There's more on this lady, I'm sure."

"Already working on it Tony. Oregon is pulling the old files together and will get back to me later today."

"Great, thanks. Jerry, anything in Tupper Lake?"

"I talked with the new project manager, McCalister. She just started on Monday. Nothing there, but she did give me the LaCroix dossier. I also spoke with the attorney who's been handling their case. Typical attorney responses, but nothing there either. Both are listed as 'sources.' I have requested a list of Resort investors, and should have that tomorrow. Tupper employees are just project and marketing people. They didn't even know who the investors were. The money people are at corporate in New York City. The attorney wasn't sure, but he didn't think there were any investors up here. We'll take a look. That's it."

"Thanks Jerry, good work with the investors thing. Keep us posted."

"Sam Perry has given us some more local manpower. Mike Murphy has been working family and friends. What have you got, Mike?"

"I'm afraid, not much. I spoke with the Kelly neighbors, nothing. This Kelly was the perfect husband and family man. The children all live out of town. One son drove up from Albany early Tuesday morning and the others should be in town this evening. Also, I did a walk around the campus of buildings here, particularly around the court. Nobody I spoke with saw or heard anything unusual Monday night. I still have a few places to visit. Finally, I visited the convenience stores that were visited on Tuesday evening by another trooper. Again nothing, but I'm going back tonight when the night crews come in. I wish I had more for you."

"It is what it is. Thanks Mike. Let's hear from forensics, Shelia?"

"Not much change from this morning. We've confirmed the only fingerprints found in the vehicle belonged to the judge. We should hear something tomorrow on DNA. I think we all know what the results will be. That's all I have."

Goss was more than a little disappointed. "One final thing," he said. "The search around the motel turned up nothing. No evidence the body was ever removed from the vehicle."

"I guess that's it people. Let's hope tomorrow is a better day. Maybe something will come from the tip line. If anybody comes up with anything, no matter how small, let me know right away. Same time tomorrow."

SEVENTEEN

ALICIA ARRIVED at Joseph's at 7:20. "Sorry, I'm late. I would have called while I was driving through Tupper Lake but I was picking up my messages. There were more than I expected, and by the time I finished there was no service again. You need to do something about that."

Cell phone service in the Adirondacks was spotty at best. In Lake Placid, Ray Brook and Saranac Lake it was fine. Two miles outside of Saranac you lost service until almost the Tupper Lake line. In Tupper Lake village, service was fine, but as soon as you left Tupper Lake there was no service again until thirty miles on the other side of Cranberry Lake. That's a fifty-mile drive with no cell service.

"I'm working on it," Joseph said jokingly. Maybe in three or four years we'll have a tower. They're looking at a couple of locations but, it's your friends at the APA that are holding it up. Talk to your buddies over there."

Alicia raised her eyebrow, but didn't reply.

Joseph was afraid the alcohol had made him a little too honest with the APA comment.

He poured Alicia a drink and refreshed his own. He thought they would talk for a while before the three-minute drive to the lodge. The two of them sat on the couch looking out at the lake. Bailey the cat sat on Joseph's lap.

"So, how's business?" Alicia asked.

"Not bad, actually. It's surprising that the markets are holding up as well as they are. Companies cut costs so much, mostly personnel, they still have strong profits. That's what's holding the market together. But, those personnel cuts were driving the unemployment rate. Still overall, I think the economy is slowly getting better. The biggest problem I deal with every day is that any bad economic news at all, and the markets have these huge swings, much bigger than normal. If you time things carefully you can realize some good gains, if you time it wrong, you're screwed. I'll tell you that I'm very worried about what's going on in Europe. Anyway, how are things with you? That must have been a shock to hear about your judge."

"It was. I've been working on this case since I moved up here. It seems to drag on and on, and here's another delay. I guess I'm just tired."

"It is only delayed a week. You'll have your decision soon enough. How do you think the new judge will rule?"

"I'm not sure."

Alicia got up and walked to the sliding glass doors to the large wood deck. She just stared at the lake and didn't say a word.

"What are you looking at?"

She shrugged, keeping her back to him.

"What are you thinking about?"

"Nothing."

She just stood there. Joseph sat stroking Bailey and watched her. Then, with a sudden jerk, Alicia turned around.

"Let's go get something to eat, I'm hungry."

Startled, Bailey jumped to the floor. Joseph gathered their jackets and they drove down Lone Pine Road, made the left on Route 3, and drove the quarter of a mile to the lodge.

Ashley greeted them as they entered. "Back so soon," she said.

Alicia looked at Joseph.

"I was here last night with my buddy Jerry," he explained. "I've told you about Jerry. He lives almost directly across the lake from me. You were staring at his house a minute ago."

"Oh, okay, I remember. Isn't he the cop?"

"I think he would prefer if you called him a trooper."

"Sure . . . trooper."

Unlike the previous night, there were several other customers having dinner. Alicia looked around the room. Many of the nicknacks had been there for more than fifty years. On one wall were five watercolors of Adirondack scenes by a local artist. Another wall displayed a dozen or so animal traps. The fireplace mantle featured a mounted red fox staring out at the dining room.

"Why do they have to do that?" Alicia asked.

"Do what?"

"Display dead animals."

"I suppose because people think they're beautiful."

"They were beautiful when they were alive. It's gross to look at dead animals, especially while you're eating."

Joseph decided to change the subject. "You never really answered my question about how you think your case is going to come out with the new judge."

"I've argued a lot of cases before Judge Pennington. He is tough, but I think he's fair. I'm a little worried because he tends to lean in favor of developers, but this case is different."

"How so?"

"This is by far the largest project ever proposed inside the Blue Line. It has enormous impact on habitat and groundwater quality. Not to mention a huge visual impact. Mt. Morris will never look the same. And the impact is not just in Tupper Lake, the entire Adirondacks will be affected. We proved that in court. The judge can't just ignore it."

"So, what if you win Alicia? What will happen to the property?"

"It will be sold, probably at auction. The developers are out of money. They can't attract any more investors or get any more financing unless they get their permits. They're already behind on their taxes."

"Do you think the public will have access to the property for hiking and stuff?" Like digging for treasure, he thought to himself.

"Depends on who buys it."

"Will it go on the market right away?"

Jerry was concerned because he had written permission to search the property with his metal detector, a permission that went along with his two-million-dollar investment. He'd told the developers it was a hobby of his to search for "treasures." The developers were glad to let him use his metal detectors on the property. The permission included a clause that said he owned anything he found.

"Why do you ask? Are you thinking of buying the property?"

Joseph laughed, "Right."

Ashley appeared with her order pad. Joseph and Alicia both ordered the salmon on rice and the house salad. They each ordered another drink as well. Over dinner, the conversation was mostly small talk. Alicia asked Joseph about his family, where he was from, and his ancestry. This was not the first time she had asked these questions and he had always either avoided them or changed the subject. Today was different. She was more persistent, and the questions were more pointed.

Other than his ex-wife, Sharon, and his best friend, Jerry, no one in his life knew of his relationship to King Joseph Bonaparte. That was not about to change tonight. Whenever he was asked about his ancestry he always replied simply that he was Corsican. Few people knew that both Napoleon and Joseph Bonaparte were born in Corte, the capital of the Corsican Republic. Everybody thought they were French.

"So you're Italian," Alicia said.

"No, Corsica was an independent republic when my great, great, great, great, grandfather, Giuseppe, was born. So I'm Corsican. In fact, the year Giuseppe was born, Corsica was taken over by France."

Using Joseph Bonaparte's given name of Giuseppe was another tactic Benton had used to avoid the subject of Joseph Bonaparte.

"I'm only part Corsican actually, Giuseppe came to America and had a daughter who married a Benton from Jefferson County. I think Benton is English." Joseph was uncomfortable with the conversation and changed the subject. "What about you, where's your family from?"

"My father was French and my mother was Scottish. I was born in Maine, but we moved to Oregon when I was only three."

After dinner, Joseph ordered another drink while Alicia sipped her wine. It was ten forty-five when they finally left the lodge and returned to Joseph's home. Joseph poured himself another drink. Alicia switched to ginger ale. The conversation had drifted to hiking in the Adirondacks.

Alicia asked if Joseph had ever done the fifty-mile hike around Cranberry Lake known as the CL50.

"Several times," he slurred. "It's a beautiful hike, but these days I prefer day hikes. My favorite hike is Ampersand. I think it's the best view in the Adirondacks." Ampersand Mountain was halfway between Saranac Lake and Tupper Lake, and had spectacular views of the Saranac lakes.

Joseph could barely get the words out.

Alicia suggested that he go to bed. "I'm going to watch the news for a while. I want to see if there's anything new about the judge. I'll be in shortly."

Joseph knew he couldn't perform sexually. He'd had too much to drink again. As he stumbled into the bedroom, he told himself he really needed to do a better job controlling his drinking. It wasn't the first time he'd told himself that. In fact, it had become almost a daily thought. "I'll do better tomorrow," had become his mantra. He never seemed to do better. Most days he drank more, and more often than not, passed out rather than going to sleep.

Alicia watched the eleven o'clock news on a Watertown station. They ran a short piece on the ongoing Kelly investigation. There were no major developments.

After checking on Joseph, she went directly to the laptop computer that sat on the credenza. When she pressed the enter button, the screen saver was replaced by the Bonaparte Coat of Arms. Two seconds later, the computer asked for a password.

EIGHTEEN

FRIDAY WAS supposed to be Jerry's day off, but as usual, he was at his desk in the Tupper Lake barracks by five a.m. While he waited for Shane Baxter to send over the Resort investor list, he would catch up on his paperwork. First, he took a quick look at the morning Saranac Lake newspaper. A front page headline talked about the lack of progress in the Kelly case. The tip line phone number was the only new information in the story. Jerry was pleased it was given a prominent position. The rest of the story was mostly speculation intermixed with a few comments from the judge's friends. A second story dealt with the simple press release from the administrative court announcing that Judge Pennington was taking over the Resort case and how the case was being delayed one week. Again, because there was little new information, it was mostly speculation.

Jerry was surprised there were no statements from anonymous sources close to the investigation. Apparently, everyone associated with the investigation was maintaining their silence. Of course, often the "sources close to the investigation" were deliberate leaks by the BCI when they wanted to release information.

It was just after noon when an e-mail arrived from Shane Baxter. As he started to scan the investor list, Jerry was amazed at the amounts of money involved. He began adding the numbers in his mind but suddenly stopped. He couldn't believe his eyes.

Matthew Jackson, Vale, Colorado, $5 million

Jefferson D. York, Savannah, Georgia, $7.5 million

Alex Smith, New York, NY, $2 million

Kendryck Starks, New York, NY, $2.5 million

David Thompson, Beverly Hills, California, $5 million

Thomas Simms, Lake Placid, NY, $1 million

Joseph Benton, Cranberry Lake, NY, $2 million

Kathryn T. Hart, Atlanta, Georgia, $4 million

Thomas Bell, Denver, Colorado, $1 million

Sharon Portman, Dallas, Texas, $5 million

Joseph Benton, Cranberry Lake, NY, $2 million. Besides being shocked at the $2 million, Jerry was puzzled and a little hurt that Joseph had neglected to tell him about his investment in the Resort.

There was not much to think about. Jerry had to disclose this to his superiors. And Joseph would have to be interviewed for the Kelly investigation. Without hesitation, Jerry printed out the e-mail, got up and walked to Station Commander Frank Johnson's office, next door to his. He stuck his head in. "Frank, do you have a minute?"

"Sure Doolin, come in. Not much on the Kelly case is there?"

"That may have just changed. I just got a list of the Resort's investors. Only two are local. But we have a problem. One lives in Lake Placid, and the other is in Cranberry Lake. My problem is that the Cranberry Lake investor is Joseph Benton, my best friend. I had no idea he'd invested in the Resort. I knew he was well off, but I didn't know he had that kind of money to put into something so risky."

Jerry handed him the e-mail. "There's one more problem. Joseph is a descendent of Joseph Bonaparte, Napoleon's older brother. You've heard of Lake Bonaparte over in Lewis County. That was once Joseph Bonaparte's property. There's a family legend regarding a treasure that Joseph Bonaparte allegedly buried somewhere in the Adirondacks. Just the other night Benton told me he is convinced it's buried somewhere on the Resort property."

"You hang around with interesting people, don't you Doolin?"

"I didn't realize how interesting." As Jerry said this, he realized how hurt he really was that Joseph had kept him in the dark. What else hasn't he told me, Jerry wondered.

"Is there any truth to the legend?" Johnson asked.

"I never believed it until I saw the evidence the other night. Joseph decoded a cipher that was in the family bible. It points to the ski area here in Tupper as the location. It sure appears there's something to it."

"We need to let Tony Goss know about this. Let's call him right now." The station commander looked at a phone list he kept on his desk and dialed.

"Tony, this is Frank in Tupper Lake. I have Jerry Doolin here in my office. Hold on one second, let me put you on speaker."

Johnson looked at Jerry as if to say, "Help me, I don't know how to put this phone on speaker?"

Jerry leaned over and pressed one button, then took the handset from Johnson and set it back on the cradle. "Tony, are you there?"

"I'm here Jerry, what do you have?

Jerry repeated what he'd just explained to Frank Johnson.

"Here's what we'll do," Tony said. "You can't go out there and do the interview yourself. But I want you there. Frank can you spare someone else for me?"

"Sure Tony, no problem."

"Thanks Frank. Jerry, I think your being there will help keep your friend honest. This may be nothing, on the other hand you never know.

What's this Benton guy like?"

"A pretty easygoing fellow. We've been best friends for almost twenty years. I certainly don't think he's capable of being involved in anything like this. But, it's been known to happen . . . ." Jerry paused and rubbed his hands over his head.

"Jerry? You still there?"

"Sorry, I'm just in a little bit of shock right now."

"Well, pull yourself together and get your ass out to Cranberry Lake. Call me as soon as you're done."

"Sure, Tony." Jerry pressed another button to hang up the phone and looked at his station commander.

"Don't look at me. You have your orders. Go. Take Jeff with you."

Jerry waited an agonizing fifteen minutes for Trooper Jeff Champlain to meet him at the barracks. He wasn't sure what he was feeling: hurt, shock, anger? For a split second he thought of calling Joseph to alert him, but of course, he couldn't do that.

"I've never told him where I have my money invested," he said to himself. "Why should he have told me? But, two million dollars . . . in one investment?"

Just then, Trooper Jeff Champlain strolled in. "Hey Jerry, you look like you're in deep contemplation. You need me to figure something out for you?"

Jerry got up and smiled, "that will be the day when I need you to figure something out for me. Let's roll."

"Where are we going?"

"Cranberry Lake, I'll explain in the car. Why don't you drive?"

"Yes sir, boss."

The ride to Cranberry Lake seemed longer than usual. The thought of being present while his best friend was being interviewed for a criminal investigation wasn't sitting well. In twenty-two years of service, he had never experienced anything like this. He hoped he was going to be able to handle it. His mind was racing. "It's probably just a coincidence. What else could it be?"

Jerry had just finished briefing Jeff as they reached Cranberry Lake. "Turn left here," Jerry said. About a quarter mile up Lone Pine Road they turned right into Joseph's driveway.

"Nice place," Jeff commented.

Jerry didn't respond, but took a few slow deep breaths as they headed up the brick walkway to the front door. This wasn't going to be easy, he thought.

Jeff knocked on the door and stood aside so Jerry could greet Joseph.

"Hey baldy, what are you doing here? I thought you were working on the missing Judge case."

Jerry was more serious than Joseph had ever seen him.

"Joseph, this is Trooper Jeff Champlain from the Tupper Lake barracks. He's working with me on the Resort case. Can we come in?"

Joseph knew something was seriously wrong. Jerry never called him Joseph.

"Sure, come on in."

In the living room, Jerry had to move some magazines to make room for himself and Jeff on the couch. Joseph sat in his easy chair.

"Joseph, this is an official visit. We're investigating the disappearance of Judge Kelly. Your name showed up on a list of investors in the Adirondack Mountain and Lake Resort."

Joseph's heart sank. He could tell his friend Jerry was hurt that he didn't know about the investment, especially after the discussion over dinner the other night. His first reaction was to get defensive.

"Look Jerry, my invest . . ."

"Joseph, stop. Let me finish. At this point, this is just a routine interview. Nobody is here to accuse you of anything. I know you've done nothing wrong. Trooper Champlain is going to conduct the interview. I can't, because we're friends. But, I'm here because I'm your friend."

Joseph remained calm and offered ginger ale to his visitors.

"Thanks, but we're fine. One more thing before Jeff gets started. I need to tell you that my superiors know everything about your family and the legend. I had no choice but to tell them. You need to answer Jeff's questions truthfully. Tell them everything, and I mean everything."

Joseph was now a bit concerned. "How much of this is going to go public? Is everything I've tried to hide about my family for thirty years going to be splashed all over the front page of the papers?"

"Absolutely not. If you're not involved with the disappearance of Judge Kelly, and I know you're not, this interview will remain confidential."

"Fair enough."

Jeff took over at this point. The questions and answers went smoothly until he started asking about Joseph's family. Joseph wasn't used to talking about this.

Finally, Jeff got to the point: "Why did you invest in the Resort?"

"I wanted to make sure I had legal access to the property. When I made the investment, I got written permission to walk the property with my metal detector, and ownership of anything I found. They thought I was a little eccentric but they were okay with it."

"Are you saying you invested two million dollars in the Resort, just to have access to their property because there *might* be a treasure buried there?"

"Not 'might.' There *is* a treasure buried there."

"Mr. Benton, where were you this past Monday night?" Jeff asked.

Joseph had to think. "I had a hamburger at the lodge. I sat at the bar, which is where I always sit when I eat alone. Ashley was tending bar on Monday."

"What time did you eat?"

"Early. I think I got there about five thirty."

"What time did you leave?"

"After dinner I had a few drinks. I think I left about eight thirty or nine."

"Where did you go when you left the lodge?"

"Straight home. I'd had a little too much to drink and fell asleep on the couch watching television."

More like passed out, Jerry thought but he was pleased that Joseph appeared to be completely open and willing to answer all Jeff's questions.

After forty-five minutes, Jeff asked the final question, "Mr. Benton, is there anything else about your investment in the resort that you should tell us?"

Joseph paused just for a moment.

"Yeah, there is something. The organization that is suing the Resort, Adirondack Environmental Watch. I have been dating the executive direc-tor for about six months now. In fact, she spent the night here last night."

"Does she know about your investment in the Resort?"

"No way."

Jerry couldn't believe what he was hearing. Is this really my best friend, he asked himself?

Joseph just glanced at Jerry. He couldn't look his friend in the eye.

"Why were you dating her?" Jeff probed. "Was it just because you liked her or were there other reasons?"

"Oh, I like her all right, but . . . okay. I thought it would be helpful to keep an eye on the opposition. Her people knew a lot about the property and I wanted to know what they knew. And, there were some nice benefits."

"I bet there were," Jerry said to himself. Joseph just sat there silently.

"And, she knew nothing about your connection to the Resort? Nothing about your investment?" Jeff pressed again.

"Nobody did. Even baldy here. My best friend. He didn't know. I'm a very private person. I don't talk about my finances to anyone."

Jeff thanked Joseph for his candor, and he and Jerry got up to leave. Joseph put his hand on Jerry's back. "Did I do okay buddy?"

"You did fine." There was no handshake and no eye contact.

As the two friends said good-bye, Jeff looked out the window at the lake one hundred fifty feet away. At the edge of the lawn, still brown from the winter, there was a dock with an aluminum boat tied to it.

"Beautiful setting. Thanks again."

Jerry looked at his watch. Ashley wouldn't be at the lodge yet. He wished they could confirm Joseph's story immediately, but he told Jeff to hightail it back to the barracks. "We have a four o'clock status meeting with the task force. Goss is going to want to hear from you regarding this interview."

Jerry was silent for the rest of the trip back to the Tupper Lake barracks.

NINETEEN

JERRY AND Jeff were on speaker phone when Tony Goss began.

"Let's get this going people. A few housekeeping items first. The media circus is growing. You've all seen what's going on down the road at the court. The good thing is we're now getting a lot of calls on the tip line. The most significant, a lady driving home at nine forty five p.m. on Monday saw two people leaving the court. She remembered it because she thought it was strange that one got in the front seat, the other in the back. She couldn't tell us much. Didn't even know if the two people were male or female. Apparently she was driving by and just got a glance. I have someone with her right now trying to get more details. It's not much, but it's something. Okay, let's go around the table and see if anybody has anything new. We'll start with Tommy."

"Thanks Tony, I've completed the review of the last five years of the judge's cases. Every APA case seems to have a little controversy. There is never an APA case that makes it to court with a happy property owner. That said, there is nothing that jumps out except the Resort case. We may have another problem on our hands. The executive director of one of the main parties to the Resort case has not been heard from today. This is the lady who called in sick yesterday. Last night she apparently left a message on the group's answering machine saying she wasn't going to be in today. I went by their offices this morning and they tried to call her at home. There was no answer, so I drove over there. No one was at home. I hope we don't have another missing person, or a runner."

Jerry jumped in. "I think I can help you there, Tommy. Jeff Champlain and I visited one of the Resort investors in Cranberry Lake today. This guy's been dating your executive director, Ms. LaCroix. She spent the night with him in Cranberry Lake last night. I bet you can find her at home right now."

"I'll head over there as soon as we're done here."

Tony Goss jumped back in. "We may be getting somewhere here. Jerry, how did your interview go?"

"I'm going to let Jeff Champlain brief the group."

Jeff explained Joseph's investment, including the story about the treasure, then gave his impressions. "The guy was completely at ease. I didn't sense any nervousness at all. Having Jerry there, I think, helped. His primary concern was confidentiality . . . not about his investment, but about this alleged treasure. I'll tell you though, this guy really believes there's a treasure. I didn't see where there would be any motivation to harm anyone. In fact, he's got as much incentive as anyone to have this case resolved as soon as possible."

"Why's that?" Goss asked.

"With the injunction that's currently in place saying no one can turn a shovel of dirt, he can't even look for his treasure. Second, any further delay puts his two-million-dollar investment at greater risk. Finally, and we haven't had time to verify yet, but Benton said he had dinner at a restaurant in Cranberry Lake Monday night and was there until nine p.m."

"Thanks Jeff. Jerry, I'm going to have Jeff take over as the Tupper Lake point man. You understand why."

"Yes sir, I do." Jerry was devastated, but he knew Tony Goss was doing what he had to do.

Goss went on, "We're going to leave this Joseph Benton and his lady friend, Alicia LaCroix, in the 'interested persons' category. I'm feeling uncomfortable with the relationship between these two. Something's not right there."

"Moving on. Shelia, anything from forensics?"

"Two things. First, we have DNA results. The blood and tissue in the vehicle does belong to Judge Kelly. Second, the blond hair found in the back seat does belong to a female, although the hair may not be as important as we had hoped. Mrs. Kelly told us they had been to dinner recently with some friends visiting from England. The friends rode in the back seat of their vehicle and the female has blond hair. We're trying to get a sample, but as you can imagine, it's going to take a while. It could be a few weeks before we have anything. That's all I have today."

"Thanks, Shelia. Mike Murphy is out interviewing our lady who called in with the tip, so I guess that's everybody. One final thing, I'm waiting until tomorrow to notify the family about the DNA results. I don't want any leaks. So far we've kept a tight ship. Let's keep it that way."

The task force meeting ended.

Jerry was feeling down after the meeting. He had never been removed from an investigation before. His friend Joseph had put him in a difficult position and there was nothing he could do about it.

On his way home, he thought about the remarkable events of the past two days. First, the revelation that his best friend might be on the trail of a family treasure worth hundreds of millions of dollars. Then his friend becoming part of a murder investigation.

His gut told him that Joseph was not involved in any murder. He thought of phoning his friend to clear the air but decided against it. He had seen that Joseph was embarrassed by the interview and everything he had to tell them. Joseph needed time to cool down and reflect, and so did Jerry.

TWENTY

VAL, BRENDAN and Judge Pennington sat with Trooper Mike Murphy around a table in the courtroom. Murphy explained that a tip had come in, "Someone thinks they saw two people leaving the court around nine forty-five on Monday evening. Then both got into what she thought was a dark colored SUV parked in the lot outside. Did Judge Kelly have an assigned parking spot?"

Val explained that there weren't assigned parking spots, but everyone always parked in the same place out of habit. She pointed out the window to an empty spot and said that Judge Kelly had always parked there.

"Did the judge have any appointments for Monday evening?"

Brendan spoke up, "No appointments. The only thing he was working on was the final decision in the Resort case. He had blocked all week to work on that."

"If he had blocked all week, why did he have to work late?"

Judge Pennington said that he knew why. "When I talked to him Monday morning he told me he was hoping to take Friday off to get his fishing gear out and go through everything. He had a fishing trip planned in a few weeks. He was almost obsessive about his fishing, and when it came to his gear, he was meticulous."

"Did he often have visitors here at the court?"

"Seldom. Every once in a while Mrs. Kelly would stop in around lunchtime and they would go to lunch. That's really it," Val said.

Pennington added, "I've known Bob Kelly for fifteen years. He has only a few very close friends, mostly his hunting and fishing buddies. I have no idea who might visit him while he was working late."

Murphy asked who was last to leave the office Monday night. Brendan said he had left around six p.m.

"Did you lock the door when you left?"

"I did. We always lock the door when there is only one person here." Brendan paused for a moment, "I just remembered something." He had completely forgotten about this. "Before I left, Judge Kelly told me he was planning on running out to get a bite to eat. I asked him if he wanted me to get something for him and bring it back before I left, he said no."

"Is there anyplace in particular he might have gone? Did he have a favorite place to eat?"

"I'd be guessing, but he probably just ran across the street to the Tail O' the Pup."

"That's probably a good guess," Pennington added.

"One final thing," Murphy said, "In the Resort case. Who would have benefited most from a delay?"

Pennington was uncomfortable with the question, "That would just be speculation," he said. "I suppose logic would suggest it wouldn't have been the Resort. Every delay costs them money. They would have liked a decision ten years ago. On the other hand, I don't see any real benefit of a delay for Adirondack Environmental Watch either. Honestly, I don't see how a delay benefits anybody."

"Can you tell me how Judge Kelly was going to rule?"

Brendan knew. He looked at Pennington for a clue about whether they should answer the question.

"I can't tell you that," Pennington said, without hesitation. "That's privileged information of the Court. This is still an ongoing case where no official decision has been rendered. No one besides Brendan knew the answer to that on Monday. Now that I've had a chance to go over Kelly's notes, I know what he was planning."

Murphy looked at Brendan, "did either side try to get you to tell them what Kelly was planning to do?"

Brendan looked at Pennington again. Pennington nodded a yes.

"Sure, both sides tried to get me to tell them. That happens in every case we have here. The attorneys are always calling before a decision is announced wanting to know which way a judge is leaning. They almost never talk to the judge. They call me, thinking I'll slip and say something that will tip them off. This case was no different. Both sides have called almost every other day for the past two weeks. They'd ask if there was anything the judge needed and then they'd probe to see if I'd say anything. The very first thing Judge Pennington taught me when I started here almost a year ago was how to deflect questions like that. You have to be an expert at that here."

Pennington held back a smile. He was proud of this young man.

Murphy thanked them all for staying late. In the parking lot, he stopped at the place Val had said Kelly always parked his vehicle. He spent twenty minutes searching the ground but found nothing.

His next stop was across the street at the Tail O' the Pup BBQ. It was a touristy place, and its proximity to the campus of state office buildings was probably the only reason it was open this time of year.

The manager told Murphy that several other troopers had come by asking the same questions. No one remembered Judge Kelly having been in on Monday.

TWENTY-ONE

TOMMY COOK had been in the investigative unit for seven years. He looked more like a businessman than a state trooper. Unlike most troopers, his sandy hair was not cut short and he sported a well-trimmed mustache and beard. It had been frustrating to him that he had not yet been able to interview Alicia LaCroix. The news that she had been dating Joseph Benton had surprised the task force and, according to Jerry Doolin, it was a relationship instigated by Benton for reasons that were far from romantic.

Cook had already been intrigued by what he knew about LaCroix and was looking forward to the interview. Although, he wished it wasn't almost six p.m. on Friday night. He had promised to take his wife to dinner in Lake Placid. A quick call home and his wife was relieved dinner was being pushed back a few hours.

Mike Murphy had gladly agreed to accompany Cook on the interview. Murphy was an ambitious young state trooper who wanted to be an investigator and transfer to the BCI. This would be good experience and Tony Goss would certainly notice. On the short ride to the LaCroix home, Murphy read her dossier provided by the folks at the Resort. Cook reminded Murphy they would not reveal to LaCroix what they knew.

"We're not going to let this lady know we have anything," Cook told Murphy. "We want to find out how forthcoming she is. Our strategy is to just let her talk."

This time, there was a car in the driveway. A Toyota Prius hybrid. "You don't see many hybrids in the Adirondacks," Murphy said. "At least, not this time of year." It was common to see summer people driving them.

Physically, Alicia LaCroix could only be described as stunning. Five foot eight, slim, but well proportioned. She had long blond hair and was clearly very fit. Her eyes were almost violet. She worked out every day and was very particular about her diet. Not a vegetarian, she was careful about the amount of meat she ate.

LaCroix looked surprised to see the two men at her door. Mike Murphy thought she was a bit nervous, but that was not unusual when two state troopers arrived unannounced. He had seen it before. Cook, on the other hand, was sure her office would have notified LaCroix he was trying to reach her. She invited the men in and they settled in the comfortable living room. LaCroix offered the two men diet cola and both accepted.

Tommy Cook explained this was just a routine visit and that all the other parties to the Resort case had already been interviewed. LaCroix seemed to relax. He continued with routine questions about the Resort case and who might benefit from the delay.

"I can't imagine anybody would benefit," LaCroix replied. "Certainly the Resort wants the case decided as soon as possible. Every day of delay costs them money. Frankly, I'm not sure they care which way the judge rules. If the judge shuts them down, they can stop the bleeding. Their investors would lose a lot of money, but at least they wouldn't lose any more. If they win, they get their financing and they can start construction."

"As for us, this has been an expensive case. At first, it was a great tool for fundraising. There are a lot of people concerned with development and they want this one stopped. Development is not just an Adirondack issue. It's a national problem. Donors around the country were willing to help fund the lawsuit. We raised millions of dollars in the early years of litigation.

Now, with the slow economy, donations have been down for the past two years and we have been spending more than we're taking in. These environmental studies have been expensive. We have had to do them, of course, to prove the Resort will permanently damage the environment. And regardless how the judge rules, we still will have appeals. The bottom line is that, at this point, nobody benefits from a delay."

"Ms. LaCroix, have you ever been arrested?"

Alicia was taken aback. She wondered if the state police would routinely do a background check on every party to every lawsuit Judge Kelly was hearing. Nonetheless, she opted to tell the truth. "Yes I have. It was when I lived in Oregon." She explained what had happened and concluded that there were a few over-zealous employees who went too far. "They paid for their mistake. I wasn't involved, so I was acquitted."

"How well do you know the developers?"

"Not well. I certainly know Shane Baxter, their lawyer. We see each other at every hearing and we've talked on the phone several times. I didn't know their old project manager too well, but I did have lunch with their new project manager earlier this week. She called me a couple of weeks ago and suggested we have lunch, so I agreed. I didn't like her much. Kind of pushy, I thought. We had lunch on Tuesday."

"Do you know any of their investors?"

LaCroix decided these troopers don't ask questions unless they already knew the answer. "Yes. I have been dating one of their investors."

"That's unusual, how did that happen?"

"He attended one of our fundraisers. It was a dinner and auction. He was high bidder on a painting. I think he bid almost twelve hundred dollars. We got talking after the event and went out for drinks afterward. A few days later he called and asked me out for dinner. We've been seeing each other ever since."

"Don't you think that's unusual for somebody to invest money in a project, and then donate twelve hundred dollars to the organization that's trying to shut that project down? Do you argue a lot over the development?"

"We don't talk about it much. A lot of couples have different views on political or social issues. This is no different."

"This is different because money is involved. Do you know how much Mr. Benton has invested in the Resort?"

"No, he's never told me. And it's none of my business so I've never asked."

"Do you know why Benton invested in the Resort?"

Cook wanted to see if she knew anything about the treasure.

"Why does anybody invest? To make money I suppose."

"Does Joseph Benton have any reason to want the case delayed?"

"You'd have to ask him. But I suspect he would like to have seen construction begin years ago."

"You haven't been in your office the past few days Ms. LaCroix, why?"

"I wasn't feeling well. I'm not sure what it was, but I just felt icky. Maybe it was just shock at hearing the news about Judge Kelly."

"How did you learn about it?"

"Judge Pennington held a conference call Wednesday afternoon with all the parties in the Resort case. He told us then. I guess between the news about Judge Kelly, and the pressure being off because the hearing is being delayed, I just needed to get away from the office."

"Where were you Monday night?"

"Here. I came home early on Monday. About three, I think. I often do that. Sometimes I work better at home. We've been getting so many calls from donors wanting to know how we thought the hearing was going to go on Monday, I needed to get away from the phones. With all the interruptions it's hard to concentrate in the office sometimes. I worked on my summation until ten thirty or so, and then went to bed."

"Did you talk to anybody?"

"I talked to the office around six. Then about nine or nine thirty, I called one of our expert witnesses to clarify something I was going to refer to in my summation."

"Did you use your land line or your cell phone?"

"I don't have a land line. I only have a cell."

Investigator Cook looked at his watch and it was almost seven thirty. "Thank you Ms. LaCroix. You've been very generous with your time. Are you going to be in your office next week in case we have some more questions?"

"Yes I will."

The two men got up and were walking to the door when Investigator Cook turned around Columbo style, "Oh, one last thing Ms. LaCroix. Where were you last evening? I came by to see you, and you weren't here."

"I was with Joseph in Cranberry Lake. He called yesterday afternoon and invited me to dinner and to spend the night. I came home this afternoon."

"Did you two discuss Judge Kelly?"

"Not really. Just a few passing comments on how tragic it is. Joseph was trying to cheer me up and I wanted to avoid the subject."

As the two men drove away they agreed that neither thought LaCroix had any motivation to delay the case.

"But, I don't know, Mike," Cook said. "There's something not right about her relationship with this Joseph Benton guy. Why would Benton strike up a relationship with the person whose major goal is to shut down the project he has two million dollars invested in? I don't get it."

Mike Murphy agreed, but he reminded Cook, "Doolin said Benton wanted to keep tabs on the opposition."

"Why, I wonder?"

"He also said that the Resort people in Tupper Lake didn't even know Benton. He wasn't keeping them informed." Murphy thought for a moment, "Maybe it had more to do with his crazy ideas about a treasure being buried on the property."

There's something not right here," Cook said. "I'm beginning to think this Benton is our guy. My gut is telling me he's a little crazy in the head. Or maybe not. Maybe he's just desperate. Two million dollars is a lot of money. Desperate people can do desperate things."

"I got the impression it wasn't the two million dollars he was concerned about. He really believes there is a treasure on that property. Two million dollars is chicken shit, this guy is worried about two hundred million dollars. You're right. This guy might be a lot more desperate than we thought."

Cook thought about what Murphy had just said. "Or a lot crazier. Maybe LaCroix and Benton are working together somehow."

"Maybe," Murphy paused, "But, I still don't see motive. Nobody can do anything on that property as long as Judge Kelly's injunction is in place. You can't begin construction on the Resort, and you can't even dig for treasure. Either way, everybody wants that case to end sooner, rather than later. Why do in the judge?"

"That's what we have to find out."

"But," Murphy added, "we shouldn't ignore the possibility that this was just a random attack by somebody looking for money."

"Sure," Cook said. "It could be. Look, we don't have anything solid here. Just a few leads and a gut feeling about LaCroix and Benton. Anyway, Tony Goss is heading this investigation and I know him well enough to know he wants something solid . . . rock solid. We still have lots of work to do."

TWENTY-TWO

JERRY WAS relieved it was Saturday. It had been a long and stressful week. A few days off were welcome. In keeping with his morning routine, he was having coffee on his porch overlooking Cranberry Lake. Being on the west side of the lake he got the early morning sun. The last week in March was still cold, but this morning brought sun and a mild temperature. Mild for Cranberry Lake in late March meant forty degrees at six thirty a.m. A heavy sweatshirt was all he needed this morning.

As he drank his coffee, Jerry thought about the remarkable events of the week—first Joseph's revelation about his family treasure, then being removed from an important investigation because of his friendship with Joseph. Maybe it was time to retire and buy a farm.

He wondered what Joseph must be feeling right now. He knew his friend felt bad about not telling him about his investment in the Resort and his relationship with the executive director of that environmental organization. Joseph had left a message on Jerry's answering machine apologizing. Jerry had heard the call come in late last night, but decided not to answer. Listening to the message this morning, he was glad he hadn't. Joseph had been drinking and the message was rambling and difficult to understand. Joseph's drinking had become a real problem. Jerry knew he needed to talk to him about it. But, for now, he wasn't inclined to return the call.

After a little housecleaning, Jerry decided to have breakfast at the Stone Manor diner. Stone Manor was the only morning gathering place in

Cranberry Lake. The lodge wasn't open for breakfast, so it was the diner where most people picked up their daily newspaper and coffee. A regular group of locals would stop by for coffee at ten and sit around to chit-chat. After coffee, they would get their paper and stop by the post office to get their mail. When Jerry had a day off, Joseph often joined him there for breakfast.

It was only nine thirty a.m., and on Saturday, the regulars didn't arrive until eleven. That was because on Saturday, the mail arrived an hour later and wasn't in the boxes until eleven forty-five. Jerry had decided on an early breakfast as he wasn't sure he wanted to chat with the regulars. If there were any other customers, they would be a random tourist or two driving through Cranberry Lake. Suzie and Jeff were the new owners of the diner and Jerry was looking forward to meeting them. As he expected, the "heart attack" breakfast perked him up. A couple of eggs, potatoes, crisp bacon, dark rye toast, orange juice and coffee could do that. It wasn't his normal healthy breakfast, but "a little treat every now and then wouldn't hurt."

He hadn't been back home ten minutes when he heard the siren at the fire hall go off. Like most fire departments in the Adirondacks, Cranberry Lake had a voluntary force and Jerry was the EMT chief for the group. Most state troopers had EMT training. Jerry had more than most. In fact, he was a paramedic and often traveled the country training others in advanced EMT and rescue techniques. He looked at his watch to make sure the siren wasn't the daily noon call.

For a split second, he thought of letting others take the call. He had trained most of the EMT's himself and he knew they could handle just about anything. Cranberry Lake had an unusually large number of certified EMT's for a hamlet its size, due in part to the tight knit community and their dedication to service, but also in part to Jerry's training of the group.

The call was probably just a backup request for the Star Lake Volunteer Fire Department, fifteen miles away.

Even while he was thinking of taking a pass, Jerry was already walking to his car to head to the fire hall. He couldn't help himself. He couldn't ever remember not going on a call if he was available. Five minutes later, he was at the firehouse. Several other people were arriving. The call was a report of a body floating in Cranberry Lake.

Two volunteers drove the ambulance and one drove the rescue truck to the town dock by the dam. Jerry drove his own vehicle. Because so many of the summer camps were only accessible by water, and the large number of recreational boaters during the summer, the department had a rescue boat. It had just been put in the water a week ago, right after the ice went out.

When the call was received by the 911 center, state police in Star Lake had been dispatched, as was the Department of Environmental Conservation whose office and dock were not far from the Cranberry Lake town dock. The docks were just a hundred yards from the dam that created the lake and a hundred yards across from the state boat launch. On the lake itself, DEC forest rangers had jurisdiction. Two rangers arrived at the dock the same time as the EMTs. In the distance they could hear a siren, a trooper arriving from the Star Lake barracks. Unlike the Tupper Lake barracks, the Star Lake barracks reported to state police headquarters in Canton, not Ray Brook.

Jerry was on site as an EMT, not a trooper. He suggested the forest rangers wait for a trooper from Star Lake while the EMTs head out to see if this was a rescue or a recovery.

The four men in the rescue boat headed south on the lake. Other EMTs were arriving and stayed on the dock as backup if they were needed. It was a sunny day and the winds were light so the lake was relatively calm. Jerry could see a fishing boat with two passengers a few hundred yards off Lone Pine Point. One of the people on the fishing boat was waving a white towel to attract their attention.

The boat slowed and Jerry saw a body floating face down in the water. As they got closer he saw there was something unusual about this body. In his experience, a floating body's arms and legs were typically positioned as though the body were trying to climb a ladder, with one arm over the head and one near the chest. Here, the arms were behind the back, being held together by what looked like duct tape. The legs appeared to be taped together as well.

No EMT training needed here, he thought. This was a crime scene. His trooper instincts kicked in. He knew the two fishermen who'd spotted the body. He asked a few quick questions and instructed them to head back to the town dock. They needed to give statements to the state police.

The DEC boat with two rangers and a state trooper pulled alongside the rescue boat. As the men looked at the grisly scene, Bob Burton, the senior ranger, was first to comment. "Somebody did a lousy job of trying to tie this guy down." Yellow rope could be seen tied around the neck and waist with about ten feet hanging loose and floating. "The ends obviously had been tied to weights of some sort to keep the body at the bottom of the lake. This body came up because it wasn't secured very well, not because of bloating. The water is much too cold," he said. Jerry jumped in the conversation, "The dive team will find whatever those ropes were tied too. The fact that this guy is dressed in a business suit suggests he was deliberately dumped here."

Jerry remembered this past Tuesday morning sitting on his porch watching something being tossed over the side of a fishing boat. He glanced to the west, caught sight of his home, and realized he might have actually witnessed this body being put in the lake.

"Look," Jerry said to everybody, "This is recovery, not rescue. It appears we have a felony on our hands. If this is who I think it is it's a big deal. We need to take our time and do this by the book. This guy's not going anywhere and he's not going to get any more dead than he already is, so there's no rush. Before we recover the body, we need to get some photos. In fact, we probably need to document the entire recovery process."

Jerry looked at the two forest rangers. He knew them well. "Guys, you're going to be turning this over to us anyway and I'm just here as an EMT, so Jim is in charge for now." He turned to the Star Lake trooper, Jim Brogan. "Jim, you have a camera in your cruiser?"

"Sure do."

"Here's what I suggest. Why don't you guys run back and get the camera. We'll stay here, protect the crime scene, and drop an anchor with a buoy to mark the site. There is probably another cruiser from Star Lake already at the dock. Let them know what we have. They'll contact your headquarters in Canton, but ask them to contact Tony Goss in Ray Brook as well. I think this may have something to do with a case they're working on. He'll want to know what we have here. Goss can coordinate with your people in Canton. We're going to need an army of dive teams, forensics people and investigators. Make sure they call the coroner too. This poor fellow is going to be taking a ride to Albany for autopsy. When you get back here we'll start the recovery and you can document every move."

Jerry then turned back to the forest rangers. "We're going to need your help today. Once we get this fellow in, we're going to need this site protected until our dive teams get here. It's going to be several hours."

The DEC boat headed back to the town dock. It was less than a ten minute ride. While one forest ranger handled the boat, the other ranger and Jim Brogan were on their radios making arrangements.

Jerry surveyed the area for floating debris. He also used the GPS device in the rescue boat to get coordinates of the site. Cranberry Lake was the result of the damming of the Oswegatchie River and had a very slight current heading north toward the dam. The buoy was gently placed just north of the floating body. He was careful not to disturb any sediment on the bottom of the lake.

Jerry wondered if the state police helicopter should be called to get a few good aerial pictures. He used his portable radio to contact Jim Brogan and suggested that Brogan have his people run the idea by Tony Goss when they talk to him.

When the DEC boat returned, it was just after noon and the sun was high in the sky providing perfect light. Once Brogan was confident he had enough pictures, the recovery operation began.

The aluminum rescue boat was equipped with a drop bow. Jerry and the other EMT's had already positioned the metal stokes basket with an open body bag so the rescue boat could "scoop" the body out of the water with minimal disturbance.

The basket was pulled into the boat. Before the bag was zipped, it was used to turn the body face up. Jerry could see the wound on the face. He had seen this type of wound before. An exit wound from a bullet. Although a formal ID would be made with scientific evidence; dental records, fingerprints and DNA, Jerry knew who this was. The body bag was zipped and the boat headed back to the dock. This was a heavy duty, porous bag that allowed excess water to drain, but even the smallest piece of potential evidence would remain inside.

Jerry's mind was racing . . . Why Cranberry Lake? Judge Kelly was shot in Ray Brook. That's where they found the bullet. How did the body get from his vehicle in Ray Brook more than fifty miles to Cranberry Lake? There must be hundreds of lakes between Ray Brook and Cranberry Lake. Any number of them would have been more remote and with fewer camps. If dumped in any of them, it could have been years before a body would be found. Why Cranberry Lake?

He thought of his friend, Joseph. Surely the investigation would now begin to focus on Joseph. The body, so close to his home—it was enough to warrant a search of his house and his boat. The boat I saw last Tuesday morning—Joseph's boat—was similar he thought. But Joseph was not capable of anything like this. Was somebody trying to frame him? Who and why?

Absolutely, Joseph would need a friend now, more than ever.

Back at the town dock, two EMTs lifted the body bag from the rescue boat to the dock. Jerry knew the coroner would simply confirm death and send the body to Albany for autopsy and forensic analysis. Facilities there were much more advanced than any local facility.

In the distance, Jerry could still hear sirens. More troopers from Star Lake were on their way. Jerry had spent seven years stationed out of the Star Lake barracks and still knew most of the troopers there.

This was now a state police investigation and Jerry's job as EMT chief was almost finished here, but there were still a few things that needed to be done. Within hours, twenty to thirty people would be in Cranberry Lake working various aspects of the case. Jerry called the president of the volunteer auxiliary and asked her if she could get some people to the fire hall to make coffee and sandwiches for the small army about to descend on the tiny hamlet.

The Star Lake barracks had a limited number of troopers and they would be focused on the investigation, so he also asked a few volunteers to stay the afternoon and block off traffic to the small access road leading to the town dock. Only those who needed access to get to their homes would be admitted.

Finally, Jerry recruited four EMTs who he knew had boats. The dive team would want a perimeter around their dive site. After all, this was a lake community and most residents had their own boats here. Not everybody had their boat in the water this early in the season, but Jerry knew if the curious couldn't get near the action in their cars, they would get into their boats. He asked the forest rangers if they could block access to the state boat launch just a hundred yards across this narrow part of the lake from the town boat dock.

TWENTY-THREE

JOSEPH DIDN'T wake up until after eleven on Saturday. Maybe it was the siren at the fire house that woke him. He was sitting in his easy chair nursing a cup of coffee and watching CNN. He wasn't really watching, he was thinking. He didn't feel very well and didn't notice the activity on the lake. He was once again thinking that he really needed to cut down on his drinking. "Maybe I should just quit the vodka and switch back to beer."

Beer had once been his drink of choice. He couldn't pinpoint when he'd made the switch to vodka. There were days he didn't drink at all. He had thought many times he wasn't an alcoholic. It was just when he did drink, he drank too much. He had asked himself the question many times before, "Why do I keep drinking when I know I've had enough? Once I start, I just can't stop."

The ringing phone interrupted his thought. He muted the TV and reached for the portable phone that was sitting on top of a pile of magazines on the floor next to him.

"Is this Timothy Benson?" a man's voice asked.

It took him a moment to remember the phony name he used when contacting the professors.

"Yes, this is Timothy."

"The caller identified himself as Chris Westbrook, the director at The Ranger School in Wanakena. "How are you Tim?"

"I'm fine Director Westbrook, and you?"

"Call me Chris, please. I've got to tell you, I was intrigued by your e-mail. I've often thought of writing a book myself but never could find the time. I envy you. I think your idea is great, everybody loves a good treasure hunt."

"Thanks Chris. It's a fun project."

"You said in your e-mail that you're in Cranberry Lake, so I thought I would give you a call. I know it's short notice, but I'm free this afternoon and thought if you wanted to come over to the school we could get some answers for you."

Joseph was excited. "That would be perfect."

They agreed to meet at one o'clock. After a quick shower and shave, Joseph sat at his laptop and typed out the questions and issues he wanted to discuss with Westbrook.

He already knew the declination shift from 1830 to 2012. That he had gotten that from the NOAA web site. And he had the formula to figure out how far off course he was. He just didn't know trigonometry.

Joseph had read a great deal about Verplanck Colvin, a surveyor who had spent years surveying the Adirondacks in the 1870s. It was his urging, along with his detailed reports to the New York State Legislature, that resulted in the creation of the Adirondack Park. Verplanck Colvin is considered by some the "Father of the Blue Line."

The remarkable stories of Colvin's visits to the Adirondacks had always intrigued Joseph. With a team of over one hundred men, Colvin had fought bears, panthers, and the harsh elements to eventually publish a number of volumes on the region's topography.

Because of his work, and the vision of the New York Legislature, the Adirondack Park is the largest wilderness area east of the Mississippi. Joseph often thought it was because of Colvin that the Adirondacks were still remote. If not for Colvin's efforts, it was likely the treasure would have been found by now.

While he was confident in the accuracy of Colvin's surveys in the 1870s, he wasn't sure about surveying techniques in the 1830s. Joseph had studied the history of the Tupper Lake area and read about the first settlement, believed to have been established around 1844 near the shores of Big Tupper Lake. Records indicated that a surveyor named Tupper had named the sprawling lake after himself in the late 1790s.

"Bonaparte would have been there around 1830. Joseph was sure he would have hired his own surveyors to mark a site where he would eventually bury the treasure without, of course, telling them his intentions.

But, how accurate were surveyors in the 1830s? All his efforts would be futile if Joseph Bonaparte's surveyors were off, even by a few degrees. The director of The Ranger School would certainly know the likelihood of their accuracy.

With his questions written out, Joseph packed up his laptop and headed to The Ranger School. As he passed the fire house and the access road to the boat launch, he noticed the fire trucks and police activity. Another boating accident on the lake, he thought.

The Ranger School was on the Oswegatchie River just south of where it enters Dead Creek Flow and Cranberry Lake.

Before entering the main building, Joseph paused to remind himself that he was the fictional author, Timothy Benson. Christopher Westbrook met Joseph in his office which looked out on the river. "Welcome to The Ranger School Mr. Benson. You look familiar, have we met before?"

"Please, it's Tim. I don't think so. Maybe we've seen each other at the lodge in Cranberry."

"That must be it. Anyway, I'm glad you could make it. This is a very interesting project you're working on."

"Thank you. It's a lot of work—a lot of research, but I am having a good time. So, as I told you in my e-mail, my major character has a compass heading from 1830. I wanted to confirm what that heading would be today. Also, how far off course would he be if he used the 1830 heading? Finally, I was hoping we could talk just a little about the history of surveying. I know it sounds like a lot . . ."

"The first two parts are easy. You already know the declination results for 1830 and 2012. The difference is $7°14'$. That means if your 1830 heading was $125°$, today you want a heading of $132.14°$. How far away did you say the target is?

"Five miles."

Westbrook tapped numbers into his calculator.

"If your protagonist used the 1830 heading of $125°$ today, and were searching an area five miles from where you took the heading, he or she would be more than a half mile off course."

"You make it look so easy."

"It's easy if you know what you're doing. Writing is probably easy for you. I struggle with that. In fact, I'm jealous of people who can write."

"Chris, how different are surveying techniques today from the 1830s? Has there been a big change?"

"The techniques are essentially the same. It's the tools that have changed. They say that surveying is the world's second oldest profession. It's been around for almost five thousand years. The Great Pyramid at Gaza was built in 2700 BC. It's 755 feet long and 480 feet high, nearly perfectly square and has a perfect north-south orientation. That didn't happen by chance. The Egyptians could establish right angles and they had a rudimentary level. The magnetic compass was brought to the west by

Arab traders in the twelfth century. Trigonometry started to come into its own in the thirteenth century. It was the marriage of measuring and mathematics that really brought surveying into its own."

"I had no idea," Joseph said. He was actually enjoying the history lesson.

"The biggest changes in the past five thousand years have occurred in just the past twenty years with the introduction of GPS and laser technology," Westbrook added. "You would be very surprised how many names of famous surveyors the average American knows."

"The only one I know is Verplanck Colvin. And, I only learned about him by researching this book."

"I'll bet you that you know several others."

"You're on."

"You ever heard of Lewis and Clark?"

"The explorers?"

"Exactly. They were surveyors. In 1801, Meriwether Lewis was private secretary to President Thomas Jefferson. Jefferson was an accomplished surveyor and he spent two years unofficially preparing Lewis for the expedition. It was Jefferson who taught Lewis the importance of keeping the detailed journals he was so famous for. Many of the Founding Fathers knew surveying techniques. You've heard of the Mason-Dixon line?"

"Of course."

"Well, Charles Mason and Jeremiah Dixon were English surveyors hired to settle the long-disputed boundaries of Pennsylvania and Maryland. The land grants overlapped. Today, the Mason-Dixon line still serves figuratively as the political and social dividing line between the North and the South."

"But probably the most famous surveyor of all was George Washington.

By the age of fifteen, Washington had studied measurement and trigonometry for surveying. For a time he was Official Surveyor of Culpeper County, Virginia. So Tim, you lose the bet. You could name a few surveyors."

"I guess I could. What about accuracy? How accurate were they in 1830?"

"Remarkably accurate, actually. The Ranger School wanted to check the accuracy of Verplanck Colvin's work a number of years ago. We were amazed at how accurate Colvin was. He would have used the same tools in 1870 as they did in 1830. Other than the declination difference, the 1830 heading would be quite accurate."

As he was leaving, Joseph took a few minutes to enjoy the river view.

He was pleased with his meeting at The Ranger School. His questions were answered, and he'd gotten an interesting history lesson. More than he had bargained for. He was confident the Spanish Royal Treasure was within his grasp. On his drive home, he decided to spend the next day walking the Big Tupper property with one of his metal detectors. He now knew where to look, and he wanted to call Jerry as soon as he got home to ask him to join the search. He was sure Jerry wasn't working on Sunday.

As he slowed to enter the hamlet of Cranberry Lake, he saw there was still a great deal of activity at the fire hall and the town dock. It must be something big. Jerry would likely be involved with whatever was going on, so the phone call would have to wait.

TWENTY-FOUR

It had been over three hours since the rescue boat had returned to the town dock with the body. The body bag lay on the dock and had not been touched. The county coroner who was coming from Canton was expected in thirty minutes. Tony Goss had arrived and Jerry was still busy making sure all the assets of the Cranberry Lake Volunteer Fire Department were available to the state police.

Jerry told Tony what he had seen early Tuesday morning while having coffee on his porch. Tony asked him to write a report and see that it got to Ray Brook early Monday morning. They walked over to the body bag together. Goss reached down, unzipped the bag and folded the corner back to reveal the head, neck and upper chest, never touching the body itself. No point in checking the wallet for identification and possibly contaminating potential evidence. Like Jerry, Goss knew full well who was lying there.

As he zipped the bag closed, both men heard the sound of a helicopter in the distance. "You took my suggestion."

"A good idea to get aerial photographs. And, the chopper was available,"

Jerry walked with Tony to his car to ride with him to the fire house. "I want one of our guys to accompany the coroner to Albany to maintain the chain of evidence," Goss said. "Maybe Star Lake can loan us somebody."

Jerry suggested they drive past the firehouse to the town beach. He wanted Goss to get a better idea where the body was found. They didn't get out of the car. In the distance they could see the DEC boat guarding the site. "Where does your friend Joseph live?" Goss asked. Jerry pointed to the left of the search boats. From this angle, the house itself couldn't be seen, but Jerry pointed to a spot about half way back from Lone Pine Point. In a hushed tone Jerry responded, "The body was found about three hundred yards off his dock." Goss suggested they drive by Benton's house. Jerry pointed out Joseph's house as they drove by without stopping. They turned around at the state camping site near the end of Lone Pine Road.

On the way back to the firehouse, Goss got on his radio and instructed the helicopter photographer to get shots of the site where the body was found, showing its relationship to Joseph Benton's house.

"By the way, does Benton have a boat?"

Jerry's heart was sinking. "Yea, he does. Looks very much like the one I saw Tuesday morning. But . . ." Jerry was quick to add, "there are hundreds just like it on the lake."

Jerry was still convinced Joseph had nothing to do with the murder. There was enough evidence for the state police to get a search warrant for Joseph's house, and Jerry was sure that would clear his friend.

On the way back to the fire hall, they saw that a crowd was gathering. Apparently the helicopter buzzing overhead had brought out even more gawkers. People were standing on the lawn behind the lodge looking out at the activity on the lake and, no doubt, spreading rumors about what was happening.

As soon as they arrived at the fire hall, Tony Goss found Tommy Cook and started giving orders. "I want you to get the DA on the phone. Tell him what we have. He may want to get out here. And we need to get someone up to Canton to get a search warrant for the Benton property, house, car and boat."

"I think they have a Town Judge here in Cranberry," Tommy suggested.

"I don't want some defense attorney saying we railroaded a local Town Justice for a search warrant. Let's do this right and get a Superior Court Judge. This is a major felony."

"Yes sir."

"I also want a cruiser down on Lone Pine Road and Route 3. Lone Pine is a dead end, so that's the only way out by car. I don't want Benton leaving. And Tommy, make sure we have plenty of lights. This will likely go late into the night."

State police divers initially had refused Cranberry Lake's offer to send three or four boats out to form a perimeter to keep the curious away. They hadn't been at the dive site fifteen minutes when they radioed the fire hall requesting four boats. Already, two pontoon boats and a fishing boat had come by to see what was happening. It could be a long afternoon of searching the bottom of the lake and they didn't need or want an audience.

They had an idea of what they were looking for, something heavy that had held the body down, maybe an anchor or cinder blocks. They were also keeping an eye out for the murder weapon. In their pre-dive briefing, they were told a slug had been recovered at the motel in Ray Brook and Judge Kelly had been shot with a single 9mm bullet.

In a private office at the fire hall, Tony Goss was meeting with the station commander from Star Lake and the zone commander from Canton. Cranberry Lake is in St. Lawrence County, and Ray Brook, where Judge Kelly's Land Rover was found, is in Essex County. There were no real issues because Goss was with the Major Crimes Unit that crossed jurisdictional lines. As a courtesy, Goss was simply bringing everybody up to speed on the investigation and the probable connection to the missing judge.

Goss was well aware of the potential upsides and downsides involved in taking the lead on a case with national media attention. If solved quickly, you're a hero. If not, the media and the public question your competence. And folks further up the chain of command feel the need, right or wrong, to make changes.

Goss next called a meeting of the Kelly Task Force to plan the forensics "assault" on the Benton property. All the major players were already present in Cranberry Lake, with the exception of the DA, Ed Reynolds. Jerry Doolin was asked to participate because of his knowledge of the house and property.

"We'll have two teams. The larger team will begin outside. Start with the boat and dock. Doolin tells me there's a lot of stuff stored under the porch. We'll take the boat to the garage for analysis. If this guy was dragged from the car to the boat, there should be plenty of evidence on the lawn and around the dock. Be careful where you walk."

Goss had asked Jerry to draw a layout of the property and house on a whiteboard. Everybody was given an assignment. A total of sixteen people would be going to the Benton home. There would be a final briefing with the entire "assault" team once the search warrant arrived.

Goss looked at his watch. It was almost four thirty. He expected his search warrant by five. "We have a few hours of daylight left," he started. "It's going to be a long night so make any calls now to let your families know you'll be home late."

He finally suggested they all get something to eat before heading out. "You probably have about forty-five minutes. The auxiliary's been cooking all day, so help yourself. I don't want anybody roaming too far away."

Jerry Doolin was feeling guilty. He had been asked to accompany the team to the Benton house to "babysit" Joseph during the search. He'd tried to get out of the assignment but Goss wouldn't budge. Of course Joseph would feel betrayed. He'd see that the search team had the complete layout of the house and property, and how they acquired it would be obvious.

While Jerry was confident the search of Joseph's home would clear him of any wrongdoing, he wasn't sure their friendship would survive.

Jerry decided to skip eating and take a walk.

The investigation was becoming focused on his friend Joseph. And worse, whose fault was that? He had to tell Goss what he'd seen last Tuesday. At least the evidence so far was circumstantial. There was no motive for Joseph to murder the judge. In fact, any delay in the Resort case, regardless of the outcome, would hurt Joseph. So who did kill the judge? And why? There were a million other possibilities. At the moment Joseph was putting his money on random robbery.

While investigators are trained to keep all possibilities open, there is always a slight tendency to focus on the wrong suspect when there is the smallest piece of evidence pointing in that direction. All of sudden, the investigators seem to grow blinders. They call it tunnel vision when they stop looking at any other possibility. Innocent people are too often convicted on circumstantial evidence because investigators focus on one piece of evidence and ignore everything else. Every investigator struggles with this, especially under the pressure of a high profile case. Jerry had no doubt Tony Goss was a good investigator and would never want an innocent man convicted. But this train was gaining steam, and it's hard to stop a train going full throttle.

He thought of sitting down with Goss but he'd be accused of clouded judgment because of his friendship with Joseph. Unfortunately, he knew that might not be an inaccurate assessment.

Jerry had twenty-two years with the state police. Maybe it was time to turn in his resignation. He really didn't want to go to Joseph's house tonight, at least not as a state trooper.

TWENTY-FIVE

JERRY DOOLIN had made his decision. He cornered Tony Goss and asked if he could have a few minutes with him privately.

They found an office in the fire hall where Tommy Cook was making calls. Goss asked Cook to find another phone and leave them alone for a few minutes.

"What's up Doolin?"

"Tony, this is hard for me to say. I've been with the force twenty-two years. I can't go with you to Benton's tonight. Joseph is my friend . . . my best friend. I don't think he had anything to do with this. Maybe my judgment is clouded. But I just can't do it. I'm going to call Frank Johnson and hand in my resignation."

Tony Goss sat quietly for a moment.

"You're an ass Doolin. You're an idiot. Don't you think I know how hard this is for you? I'm not an insensitive fool. You're not giving anybody your resignation tonight." Goss leaned forward. "Look Jerry, you and I have known each other a long time. If you want to help your friend, you need to be there when we execute this warrant. I don't know if your friend has anything to do with this or not. But I do know that I have a great deal of respect for your judgment. You know this guy. I can't ignore your opinion."

Jerry shook his head. "No can do, Tony."

"I'll make a deal with you Jerry."

"What's that?"

"Play devil's advocate. I want you to question everything we do, every-thing we find. This Benton guy is lucky to have a friend like you. But, if you really are his friend, don't abandon him when he needs you most. You're going to tell me why this guy is innocent."

Jerry thought for a long moment. Finally he nodded. "Okay Tony, you've got a deal."

As they started to leave, Tony put his hand on the door knob, held the door shut and turned. "Jerry, I admire what you're willing to do tonight. This entire conversation is between you and me."

"Understood."

"And one more thing, I know I don't have to say it but, while you're in that house you're a state trooper. I expect you to act like one."

"Of course."

Tony Goss found his team leaders and ordered them to get everyone together for the final briefing. "Ten minutes," he said. It was five thirty and he was beginning to worry about losing daylight.

Jerry was relieved. Joseph wouldn't understand, and he couldn't tell Joseph what his role really was. At least not now. It was a tough decision, but Tony was right. Being on the inside was the only way to help. More important, it was the right thing to do.

Sixteen people in eight vehicles headed to the Benton house. Jerry Doolin rode in the lead car with Tony Goss and went to the front door with him while the others gathered their equipment.

Joseph opened his door, looked at Goss and Doolin and looked up at the cars on the road. "What's going on here?"

"Joseph, this is Sergeant Tony Goss. He's the senior investigator for our Bureau of Criminal Investigation. We have a search warrant. Can we sit down?"

The three men sat in the living room. Through the sliding glass doors to the deck, Joseph could see state troopers walking toward his dock.

"What's this all about Jerry?"

"Joseph, Judge Kelly's body was found in the lake this morning."

Benton turned around and could see the rescue boat and several other boats still out on the lake.

"So that's what all the ruckus is about. You think I had something to do with it?"

"You're an investor in the Resort and his body was found just a few hundred yards from your house. We're just doing our jobs."

Jerry knew how shallow his words sounded. Joseph looked stunned. Before he could respond, there was a tap on the door. Goss got up and let three men and two women in to begin their work.

"Tell these people to be careful coming in and out of the house," Joseph said. "If Bailey gets out, I'm suing somebody." Bailey had been with him since she was a kitten. Other than Jerry, Bailey was Joseph's only real friend. Or maybe Bailey was his *only* friend.

While Goss was talking to one of the forensics people who'd just come in, Joseph whispered to Jerry. "You're a cop through and through aren't you, asshole? I thought you were my friend! You know I didn't have anything to do with this. Can I at least get myself a drink?"

The comment was like a fishing knife plunging into Jerry's stomach.

"Joseph, listen to me. I am your friend. And, you're right, I'm also a cop. I have a job to do and I'm going to do it. As your friend, I'm going to tell you not to drink right now. You need to stay sharp tonight. I don't expect them to find anything, and this will be over in a few hours. They may take a few things for further analysis, but everything will be returned. The best thing you can do is to cooperate in every way you can."

"You asshole, I listened to you the other day and told your buddy everything. Stuff I've keep secret for thirty years. And what did that get me? A whole army of assholes going through my house. I want to see the search warrant."

Jerry handed Joseph a copy of the search warrant.

Joseph went to the kitchen and made himself an extra large drink. He looked around for Bailey, but figured she was already hiding under the bed.

Goss walked over and sat next to Jerry. "You're doing great. When this is all over your friend will thank you."

"I'm not sure about that," Jerry said.

"Hang in there."

Tony Goss went outside to see how the forensics people were doing with the boat. They had found traces of blood in the boat. "It could just be from fish," one of the investigators told Goss. "A quick look under the microscope will tell us. Of course, it could even be Benton's. He may have cut himself fishing. It happens every day."

"We'll know soon enough," Goss said. Tony Goss noticed the rope tying Benton's boat to the dock was yellow nylon, similar to the rope tied around the body. "I want samples of that rope."

"We've already got it. There was about fifty feet of it hanging in that shed over there. We found a roll of duct tape and a dozen cinder blocks, too. We'll take a few of the cinder blocks in case the dive team finds anything. Maybe they can be matched."

"How much longer?" Goss asked.

"Another hour or two, maybe more. I want to get samples from the bottom of the boat while we're here. That way, nobody can claim anything was contaminated in transit."

"Take your time, there's no rush."

It was beginning to get dark and two troopers were setting up flood lights on the dock, powered by a generator that had been set up on the road. Two other forensics people were checking the path from the front of the house to the back. Numbered markers indicated where items had been collected. A photographer was taking pictures.

Inside, Joseph and Jerry sat together in silence. Joseph was on his second drink. The computers had been packed and removed, leaving disembodied computer screens, keyboards and disconnected wires. Four banker's boxes stood open on the floor by the desk. Two were full of files from the desk drawer. A trooper was making an inventory of each file as it was placed in the box.

Goss asked Jerry to step outside. "Is your friend a fisherman?"

"I don't think he even owns a fishing pole."

"We haven't found any fishing gear. If he doesn't fish, why own a boat?"

"Lots of people on the lake don't fish. They just like to be on the water. Sometimes Joseph and I take his boat to the Pinecone in Wanakena for dinner. During the summer, these restaurants on the lake can have as many people arrive by boat as by car. If you live on the lake, it's not unusual at all to have a boat and never fish."

"Do you know . . . does he ever lend his boat to others who might use it for fishing?"

"I doubt it. He's not real friendly with his neighbors. He's a very private person. He doesn't have a lot of friends."

"Heavy drinker?"

"Yea, he's got a problem."

"Blackouts?"

"Not that I know."

"Jerry, what we're finding here doesn't look good. We should finish up here in an hour or so. I'm ordering twenty-four-hour surveillance. We should know by mid-morning if we're going to bring this guy in for some hard questioning. I'm sorry. It's beginning to look like Joseph might be our guy."

"Just remember, everything you have is circumstantial. It could be a setup."

Goss nodded and replied half-heartedly, "It could be."

Jerry sat alone on the front step to think. The sun had gone down and it was getting chilly. It had been a clear day and Jerry could see a few stars in the evening sky.

What's going on here, he wondered. *Something is not right.*

Jerry could not believe his friend was capable of murder.

TWENTY-SIX

JERRY STOOD outside and watched as the teams finished their work. The boat had been secured on the state police trailer, covered with blue plastic and tied down for the trip to Ray Brook. At the end of Lone Pine Road, four of the vehicles, including the SUV with the trailer and boat, turned right toward Ray Brook. From there, everything collected would be carefully packed and sent to the forensics lab in Albany. The other four vehicles turned left for the short trip back to the firehouse. A new, unmarked vehicle was parked on the road where it would remain through the night.

Jerry was again riding in silence with Tony Goss. As they passed the lodge, they saw that the media had moved their encampment from Ray Brook to Cranberry Lake. The lodge parking lot was full and in the small lot at the adjacent town beach, four satellite trucks faced forward, their dishes pointed skyward.

Goss slowed the car to view the spectacle. "Vultures," Jerry said.

"I couldn't agree more. Nonetheless, I'm going to have to make a statement to them tonight."

At the fire hall, Jerry was not surprised to see a few auxiliary ladies were almost finished cleaning the kitchen.

"There's fresh coffee," someone yelled.

"The hall's available as long as you need it, Tony."

"We'll be finishing up here shortly," Goss told Jerry. "I'm heading down to brief the press shortly. Why don't you go home? You look exhausted."

Jerry shrugged, "Let's talk in the morning."

Exhausted wasn't the word. Numb was more like it, Jerry thought as he drove home. The dark house felt emptier than usual as he sat in his easy chair. He never even turned on a light.

His thoughts were jumbled. One way or another, I lost my best friend tonight. Whether or not he's guilty of murder, he'll never forgive me for being part of the investigation."

He tried to focus on the evidence, but it was starting to make his head hurt. This isn't right. No motive. Every crime has motive. He thought through what he knew; the Resort investment, the alleged treasure, the Big Tupper property, the girlfriend, Alicia. Nothing pointed to a motive for murder. But, he pinpointed what was bothering him most: Why bring Kelly to Cranberry Lake, dead or alive?

Still, the growing mound of evidence worried him. Blood in the boat, yellow rope, duct tape. If there's a match, Joseph's in big trouble.

Suddenly, Jerry wondered what they might find on Joseph's computer. Who knew how his finances were? No matter how deep in the hole Joseph was, he couldn't see how killing Judge Kelly could change that.

Jerry felt he was losing his focus. There were too many things to think about. He decided to make a sandwich and turn on CNN to see if they were going to carry the press briefing live. The murder of a judge in the Adirondacks had become national news.

Scrolling from right to left across the bottom of the screen was the alert, "New York State Police briefing in missing judge case expected this hour." In a small box in the upper right hand corner of the screen was the picture of an empty podium and microphones. Jerry settled in with his sandwich and diet cola and listened to the other news while he waited for Tony Goss to appear.

The phone rang. Jerry decided not to answer, but he couldn't help hearing the message as it was being recorded. "Hey, you asshole, I hope you know you ruined my life and everything I've worked for these past thirty years." The words were slurred. "You know there's a cop sitting outside my house. I know you're listening you asshole. I'm glad you're not picking up. I didn't want to talk to you anyway. You bald-headed jerk."

Jerry had mentally prepared himself for the call. He was glad he didn't answer. He never liked talking to Joseph when he was drunk anyway.

The press conference hadn't started when he finished his sandwich. He put the TV on mute and sat at the kitchen table to outline the Kelly case on paper.

He followed his usual process, first writing down the evidence and events that pointed to guilt, then the events and evidence pointing to innocence. When he was finished, the guilty side of his sheet was full. There was only one word with a big question mark on the not-guilty side.

Motive?

He looked at the TV screen and turned the sound back on. A female announcer was interrupting a debate about the federal budget, "Let's listen as the New York State Police bring us up to date on the new developments in the missing judge case in the Adirondack Mountains." The little box became full screen right on cue.

My name is Sergeant Anthony T. Goss and I'm the senior investigator in the Judge Robert Kelly investigation. I have a brief statement and will not take any questions tonight.

With help from the Cranberry Lake Fire and Rescue, a body was recovered this afternoon from Cranberry Lake. There has been no positive identification. The body has been transported by the St. Lawrence County coroner to the New York State Police forensic facilities in Albany, New York. Identification, autopsy and forensics will take place there. We don't know if there is any connection between today's recovery and the Judge Robert Kelly case. That's all I have for you tonight.

Thank you.

As Goss walked away from the microphones, reporters surrounded him, yelling questions. CNN stayed with their live shot. "Was the body Judge Kelly? Was the body male or female? Has the Kelly family been notified? Do you have any suspects in the Kelly case? Whose home were you searching? What did you find?"

Goss walked away without saying a word and the screen switched back to the female announcer at the Atlanta news desk. "The New York State Police aren't confirming anything except that a body has been recovered in the remote hamlet of Cranberry Lake in the Adirondacks. Sergeant Anthony Goss, who is the senior investigator in the mysterious Judge Kelly case, would not make any connection between that case and today's recovered body. Let's go back live to Cranberry Lake and Timothy Cole. Tim, what have you learned?"

Kathy, this little hamlet has been taken over by New York State Police today. As you just heard, they are not ready to make any connection between the discovery of a body today and the Kelly case. I can report, and multiple sources have confirmed, the body recovered this afternoon was a male in a business suit.

We also have learned a home on the east shore of the lake was searched today and a number of items were taken, including computers and a boat. Finally Kathy, a source familiar with the case tells me there may be an arrest in the missing judge investigation as early as tomorrow. In Cranberry Lake, New York, this is Timothy Cole.

Jerry Doolin clicked off the TV and sat with his eyes closed.

TWENTY-SEVEN

THE STORY was splashed over the front page of every Sunday paper in the North Country. Unlike the earlier Kelly stories, these were full of "facts" that allegedly came from "sources close to the case." Every paper suggested an arrest was expected shortly.

The evidence collected at the Benton home and recovered from the lake had been transported to the state police labs in Albany Saturday night. Typically the evidence would wait for analysis to begin on Monday, but an entire team of forensic specialists had been called in to work on Sunday.

The dive team had found four cinder blocks and a 9mm Beretta pistol in the lake. There were no fingerprints on the gun. Ballistics testing would take place as soon as the gun was completely dried out and deemed safe to fire. The cinder blocks appeared similar to those found in Benton's shed. Analysts would likely be able to determine if the cinder blocks recovered in the lake and those found at the Benton home were made at the same time and at the same plant.

Duct tape from the body would be checked for a match with the duct tape found at the home. It would be relatively easy to find a piece of tape from the body where one end matched the tear from the end on the roll found at the house. More difficult would be the analysis of the tape itself. Fingerprints could be left on the adhesive. Fiber or other material could also have been picked up as the tape was torn. It's not unusual for the adhesive side of tape to touch the leg or shirt of the person using it, picking up fibers from their clothes. Investigators knew the tape often collected some of their best evidence.

The rope would be checked for a match with the rope found at the home. The contents of the bottom of the boat had been collected. Even the smallest piece of material found in the boat would be analyzed. Computer specialists had been called in to begin going through Joseph Benton's digital files.

The hardest part of the investigation for Tony Goss was waiting for forensics results. The wait was necessary. He didn't want to hear maybe. He wanted hard facts. He was famous for asking, "What do we think, what do we know and what can we prove?"

Goss was at his desk by six forty-five Monday morning. One way or another, it was going to be an eventful week.

Confirmation had come in overnight that the fingerprints on the body matched Judge Kelly. Enough for positive identification. The lab was still doing DNA comparisons with hair samples obtained from his home, but that would just confirm what they already knew. The preliminary report showed death resulted from a single bullet to the back of the head. The blood found in the boat was human. A DNA match with Kelly would take several more days.

A call came in at seven forty-five.

"Sergeant Goss, this is Alicia LaCroix. I'm the executive director of Adirondack Environmental Watch. We're one of the parties in the Resort case Judge Kelly was hearing."

"I know who you are, Ms. LaCroix. How can I help you?"

"I saw you on the news the other night and they said you had searched a home in Cranberry Lake. The papers said it was Joseph Benton's home. As I told one of your officers the other day, I had been dating Joseph for about six months. I spent the night at his house last Thursday."

There was a pause. "Yes, Ms. LaCroix."

"Well, I never imagined Joseph was capable of such a thing. I'm worried. Am I in any danger?"

"Why would you think you are in any danger?"

"If he murdered a judge and everything, maybe . . . well you know. Is he going to be arrested today?"

"Ms. LaCroix, you're an attorney. You know I can't comment about an active investigation. Let me ask you a question. Let's just suppose this Mr. Benton is involved with the Kelly case, do you know of any reason he might want to hurt the judge?"

"I have no idea. Maybe something to do with the Resort or something."

"All right, Ms. LaCroix. We may want to talk to you again in a few days. This investigation is far from over. In the meantime, if you feel as though you're in any danger, you need to do whatever you think you have to, in order to protect yourself."

"Thank you Sergeant."

"Thank you Ms. LaCroix."

"That was strange," Goss said to himself as he hung up the phone. "What's she fishing for? Maybe she's working with Benton and trying to find out how much we know. Maybe they're getting ready to run."

A note had been placed on his desk while he was on the phone. The trooper stationed outside Benton's home reported that Benton had not left the house since Saturday night.

"At least he's making it easy for us."

Goss called Jerry Doolin in Tupper Lake to brief him on the developments since Saturday.

"I watched your briefing on television Saturday night," Jerry told him.

"You did a good job."

"Thanks. They say everybody gets their fifteen minutes of fame. I got about fifteen seconds. I feel cheated. Look Jerry, I'm calling for two reasons. First, I want to thank you and everybody at the fire hall for your hospitality on Saturday. You've got a great group of people there. They're very professional."

"Thanks Tony. They're good, dedicated people."

Goss brought Jerry up to date. The evidence against Joseph was building. "By the way," he added, "I got a call a little while ago from Joseph's girlfriend."

"Really, what did she want?"

"She wanted to know if Joseph was going to be arrested today. She said her reason for calling was she was worried she might be in danger. She was looking for information, Jerry. How much do you know about her?"

"Nothing really, I never met her. I didn't even know they were dating until Joseph told Jeff Champlain and me the other day. I knew he was seeing someone, but I didn't know who."

"I think Benton might have an accomplice. Let's talk about this later. I've got to run. I've got two people waiting at my door."

"Thanks for the call Tony."

Jerry thought the LaCroix call to Goss was odd, and wondered if she and Joseph had cooked up some scheme together. Did Joseph tell her about the treasure? Did they decide they needed to convince the judge to delay the case, then their plan went bad? But Jerry was convinced there was no way Joseph would have told anybody about the treasure, especially someone he only met six months ago.

Shelia Kenyon from forensics knocked on Goss's door. "Tony, do you have a minute, I've got something for you."

"I hope it's a cup of coffee?"

"No, but I'll walk down the hall with you if you are going to get one."

"Sounds like a plan."

Tony got up and they both headed for the break room.

"We've got matches on the rope and duct tape as well as debris from the bottom of the boat. There's no question Kelly's body had been in that boat."

"The clothes also indicate the body was dragged from the driveway to the dock. We've still got a lot to do, but you have more than enough to bring this guy in for some more questioning."

"Good work Shelia. Let me buy you a cup of coffee."

"No thanks, I don't touch the stuff."

"With the hours you keep, how do you function without coffee?"

"I'm high on life Tony. I don't need drugs to keep me going."

"Yea, right."

"I'm going to call Eddie in Elizabethtown and let him know we'll be bringing Benton in. He may want to come over and watch the fireworks. Thanks for the good work."

Goss took his coffee back to his office and called Sam Perry, the station commander, and requested a couple of troopers to head out to Cranberry Lake to bring Joseph Benton to the Ray Brook barracks.

After the troopers left, Goss called Jerry Doolin.

"Jerry, Tony here, I wanted to let you know, we're picking up your friend Joseph. We're bringing him in for questioning. There are matches on everything, the rope, duct tape, fibers, everything. I'm sorry. This guy is going to have a long day answering questions."

"I understand, but what was his motive?"

"You don't give up do you?"

"Tony, I've known Joseph Benton for twenty years. I don't believe he's capable of murder. Somebody's setting him up. Maybe this LaCroix lady. I don't know why, but something's not right here. There's no motive."

"We'll find the motive Jerry. Everything points to him. Our guys will be getting into his computers today. Maybe we'll find something there. And, who knows, he may be working with LaCroix."

"Look Tony, I understand you don't have a choice about bringing him in. I don't have a problem with that. But something's not right here. I'm going to continue being your devil's advocate."

"That's fine Jerry. You do that. And I'm going to continue doing what I have to do."

The conversation ended.

Jerry looked at the legal pad and the notes he had written Saturday night. Under the word "Motive" he wrote "Alicia LaCroix?"

TWENTY-EIGHT

JUDGE PENNINGTON, Val and Brendan were sitting in Pennington's office talking about the events of the weekend. Val had not slept well, and her eyes were bloodshot. Brendan had never experienced the death of someone he was close to.

"I talked with the senior investigator in the case this morning." Pennington told them what he learned. "I also spoke with Sadie Kelly. The family is holding up as well as can be expected. All the children are home and they are giving Sadie a great deal of comfort. The state police can't tell us when they'll release the body, so there are no funeral arrangements yet."

"Val, are you all right? Do you think you should be here?"

"Honestly, I don't think so, Judge. I have some vacation coming. Would you mind too much if I took the week off?

"That's fine Val. Why don't you go home. What about you Brendan?"

"I'll be okay Judge. We have a lot of work to do if we're going to be ready for the Resort hearing next week."

Pennington was pleased and once again he thought Brendan more mature than his age.

They were interrupted by the phone. Brendan answered and listened as the caller explained the state police were close to making an arrest in the Kelly case. "Is Judge Pennington available for comment?"

I'm sorry," Brendan said. "Judge Pennington has no comment. He won't be talking to the press today."

Pennington knew who was on the other end of the line. He smiled. "Thanks, I really don't want to deal with them today."

"Don't worry Judge I'll take care of it. By the way, do you have any idea who this guy is they're planning to arrest?"

"I'm not sure they're getting ready to arrest anybody. I think the press is just testing us to see if we'll say anything."

Brendan spent a good part of the rest of the day answering the phone and dealing with the media. He remembered several of the reporters from the week before.

Judge Pennington started reading environmental impact studies. At about two p.m., a package was delivered to the front desk where Brendan was answering calls. He signed for it and took it into Judge Pennington.

Pennington looked at the return address. The Adirondack Mountain & Lake Resort. "I almost forgot," he said. "The motion for permission to present new evidence." He opened the package and pulled out a two sentence cover letter, the five page motion, a transcript, an affidavit signed by Maureen McCalister, and an audio cassette.

Reading the brief, Pennington was not surprised at the quality of the writing. Most the Resort briefs he had read over the weekend had been some of the best he had ever seen. "This Baxter is a good lawyer and a good writer."

Pennington called Brendan into his office. "Do we have a cassette player around here?"

"Sure Judge, I'll bring it in."

Pennington let Brendan read the motion while he set up the cassette player. When Brendan was finished, they both listened to the short tape.

"Wow," Brendan opined. "A little arrogant, isn't she?"

"That's more than a little arrogant, Pennington responded. "LaCroix is really something. I can't wait for her response. She's going to fight like hell to keep this out of the record. Her brief will be a classic."

Brendan thought about Judge Kelly. "Judge Kelly would have been pissed at this."

"You bet he would. He would have been really, really pissed. Can you imagine how he would have responded? He would have torn the lady's head off in court."

"What are you going to do?"

"I'm going to wait to see what she has to say for herself. I owe her that. That said, I can't imagine what she'll say. No doubt, she'll come up with something creative. She's a good lawyer."

Brendan was embarrassed he had asked the question. Of course the judge wouldn't make a decision without giving the other side a chance to respond, he thought.

Pennington went back to his work. He still had a lot of reading to do. While he would probably use Judge Kelly's draft brief as a foundation, he would add his own thoughts. From what he had read so far, Judge Kelly's draft ruling was spot on from a legal perspective.

The written ruling was one thing. What he would say from the bench was something altogether different. Of course, the bottom line would be the same. The written ruling would provide the legal foundation for his decision. From the bench he could express more of his personal opinion. He was beginning to suspect that one of the parties in this case was going to receive a verbal lashing from the bench. A verbal lashing like he had never given before.

TWENTY-NINE

IN PAJAMAS and robe, his hair askew, a bloody-eyed Joseph opened his door to a pair of troopers at eleven a.m. "You guys again. What, did you forget something? Where's your buddy Doolin? Sleeping late this morning?"

The troopers didn't respond to Benton's questions. "Mr. Benton, Senior Investigator Goss wants to ask you some questions."

"Fine, where is he?"

"He wants to see you in Ray Brook. You can ride with us."

"Where's Doolin? I want to talk to Jerry. What's going on here?"

"Will you accompany us to Ray Brook?"

"Sure, sure. I've got nothing better to do today than answer your ridiculous questions. Is this come as you are, or will you let me get dressed?"

On the ride to Ray Brook, it occurred to Joseph that all this murder stuff started to come down *after* his dinner with Jerry. The dinner at which he told him *exactly* where the treasure was hidden.

From the back of the state police cruiser, Joseph started yelling. "That asshole set me up. He's planning to steal it, my entire heritage. He's not a fucking cop, he's a thief."

At Ray Brook, apparently no one was in any hurry to begin the questioning. Waiting in a locked interrogation room, Joseph's anger grew as he tried to unravel exactly how Jerry Doolin planned to go about stealing his treasure.

"That asshole needs to be stopped."

Finally, Goss entered the room, accompanied by Thomas Cook.

"Sorry to keep you waiting Mr. Benton," Cook said.

"Yeah, yeah." Joseph said. "Hurry up and wait. Let's get this over with."

Tommy Cook told Joseph the interview was being recorded. "Do you have a problem with that?"

"Whatever. If you want to know how that body got in the lake, I can tell you."

"Really. Go ahead and tell us, Mr. Benton," said Goss."

"It was one of your own. You probably won't do anything about it but, it was one of your own."

Goss was intrigued, "One of our own? Would you care to tell me who?"

"That fuck, Doolin, who else? All this started happening when I told him I'd figured out where my treasure was buried. He's trying to make it look like I did something to that judge. You know, get me out of the way so he can steal it. You need to arrest that asshole. He's a thief and a murderer."

"When did you tell him about the treasure?"

"We had dinner last Wednesday. That's when I told him."

Goss smiled. "Mr. Benton, that's an interesting theory. There's one small problem. Judge Kelly went missing Monday night. Unless Jerry Doolin has some magical powers and knew what you were going to tell him on Wednesday, I don't think he would have done anything to the judge two days earlier. Are you aware of Sergeant Doolin having any magical powers?"

Joseph was so angry, he'd never considered the timeline. He'd had dinner with Doolin on Wednesday. Friday, Doolin showed up with a trooper asking questions. Saturday, they pulled a body from the lake a few hundred yards off his dock. As Goss's comments sank in, Joseph was a little embarrassed. And the sarcasm from Goss made him furious.

"If we're done with this fantasy, can we get down to business?" asked Cook.

"This is a set-up. I've been framed by Doolin. You need to stop him. I don't know how he knew, but he knew."

"Mr. Benton, who else did you tell about this so-called family treasure?"

"Nobody, that's how I know it was Doolin."

"When did you tell Ms. LaCroix?"

"What are you talking about? Never. I never told her. I never told anybody except Doolin."

The questioning went on for more than four hours. Goss and Cook took turns. While one was asking questions, the other would often leave the room. As the afternoon went on, the questions from Goss became more pointed. Tommy Cook remained the good guy and while Goss was out of the room he would tell Joseph that Goss was getting impatient and urged Joseph to be more forthcoming.

Finally, Cook put his hand on Joseph's shoulder. "If you tell us what really happened, I may be able to convince the district attorney to give you a break. Remember, this is a death penalty case."

"I am telling you. I've been telling you all day. I don't know what else you want."

Meanwhile, Goss would consult with Edward Reynolds, the district attorney who had been observing the interview from another room. Reynolds would often suggest a line of questioning for the next round.

The investigators left Joseph alone at the end of the day for more than an hour while Goss and Cook reviewed the day's forensic test results with Reynolds.

Joseph had been in the room for more than seven hours. Apparently, they weren't letting him go home. The same questions were asked over and over. Phrased differently, and repeated by both Goss and Cook. He'd figured out hours ago that Goss was playing "bad cop," while Cook was playing "good cop.'

Time to bring this to an end, Joseph thought. In light of the new forensic results, Goss, Cook and Reynolds were thinking the same thing . . . for very different reasons.

Goss looked at the other two men. "All right, gentleman, one last time, what do we think, what do we know, what can we prove?"

They each gave their final impressions. District Attorney Reynolds was the last of the three to speak, "there's plenty of evidence for a conviction. It's circumstantial, but it's a lot, and it all points to Benton. I am a little uncomfortable with the fact we don't have any idea why he did it. Albany is still going through his computers and something may come up there. If we can't show why he did this, a good defense lawyer may be able to create just enough doubt for a jury to acquit. Bottom line? I would feel better if we had a motive."

Goss made the decision. "Let's not move too fast on this. We know a lot, but there's too much we don't know. I want to bring in this LaCroix woman. My gut tells me her phone call this morning had nothing to do with her safety. Let's push her a little and see what she knows. They could be working together."

Tommy Cook made arrangements for Benton's transportation back to Cranberry Lake and continued surveillance.

They would call LaCroix at her home at seven a.m. and invite her to come in before she went to her office. If she was working with Benton, and the invitation to answer a few questions caused her to run, they would be prepared. A surveillance team would be at her home by five a.m.

THIRTY

ALICIA LACROIX was up early, thinking about the motion to admit new evidence that had arrived at her office the day before. After listening to the tape that accompanied the motion, she was furious at Maureen McCalister for recording their lunch conversation.

In the shower she thought about that lunch and remembered how tired she had been. She hadn't gotten any sleep the night before. Not only had she been tired, she'd been on edge. "It's my own damn fault for shooting my mouth off."

She'd just emerged from the shower when Tony Goss phoned, requesting she stop by the Ray Brook barracks for a few questions.

It was eight fifteen a.m. when Alicia LaCroix left her home. An unmarked car followed her at a discrete distance.

LaCroix was offered a seat in the same room Joseph Benton had been in the day before. She refused an offer of coffee. Goss thanked her for coming in and apologized for the short notice."

LaCroix stood to shake his hand.

"I believe you've met Tommy Cook."

"Yes I have, good morning."

The first hour covered the same ground Cook had explored in his previous interview with LaCroix. There were more pointed questions about the Oregon incident a decade earlier.

"Your employees were convicted for spiking those trees. Why did they do that?"

"The property was being cleared for development. They were old-growth trees and I guess they thought spiking them would stop the cutting. They were over-zealous, they were wrong, and they paid for their mistake."

"Was it a development like the Adirondack Mountain and Lake Resort?"

"It was not as large, but they were old-growth trees, so it could be argued that more sensitive habitat was being destroyed."

Goss decided to change the subject.

"Ms. LaCroix, when we spoke yesterday, you said you were concerned for your safety. Do you still feel that way?"

"Yes a little."

"When I asked you why Joseph Benton might want to harm Judge Kelly, you thought it might have something to do with the Resort. Can you tell us why?"

"I don't know. He donated twelve hundred dollars to an Adirondack Environmental Watch fundraiser to help pay for our lawsuit. I guess that was it."

"What other involvement did he have in the Resort?"

"I'm not aware of any other involvement he would have."

"Did he have any particular interest in the property?"

"Actually, when we had dinner the other night, he was asking what would happen to the property if we won the case and the development was stopped. I asked if he was thinking of buying it. I was joking, of course."

"What did he say?"

"He laughed and said no."

"Why do you think he was so interested in the property?"

"I have no idea. Maybe he was just making conversation. But I sensed there was more to it."

"Why'd you sense that?"

"Maybe it was his tone of voice. Maybe it was because we seldom talked about the Resort or the lawsuit. The questions were a bit of a surprise."

"Does he have the resources to buy that property?"

"You would have to ask him. I have no idea what his resources are. I know he has a little money. He has a beautiful home on Cranberry Lake. Look, are we almost done? If not, I need to call my office."

"We've got some more questions Ms. LaCroix. We may be here for a while."

"This is taking a lot longer that you told me this morning. Am I a suspect in this case?"

Tony Goss smiled, "First, I don't recall saying how long we would be. And, why would you think you are a suspect?"

"I thought you just had a few questions. I didn't think we would be here all morning. I have a lot of work to do today." Alicia was thinking about her response to the Baxter motion. It was due in court by Friday. She didn't want to wait until the last minute. She needed to keep this recording out of the record.

"Okay, Ms. LaCroix. Let's take a break. Call your office. While you're doing that, can I get you anything? Water, soda, juice?"

"A bottle of water would be great," she said.

Goss, Cook and Reynolds stepped outside to discuss strategy. "A cool customer," Reynolds began. Cook agreed, "Or a really good liar. But I don't think she knew anything about Benton's treasure." Tony Goss wasn't so sure.

§

"Ms. LaCroix, I want to talk a little more about your relationship with Mr.

Benton," Goss said gently. "How close were you two?"

"I'm getting the impression you guys think this was more than it really was. Joseph and I had dinner a number of times. I spent a few weekends in Cranberry Lake. That was about it. I was seeing other men, and I assume he was seeing other women."

"You were intimate weren't you?"

"That's really none your business. But yes, we were."

"Do you know what his source of income is?"

"Not really. He always said he was a financial analyst. He never talked about clients or anything like that, so I just assumed he had money and spent his time analyzing his own investments. Kind of like a day trader."

"Do you have any idea what he was worth?"

"I already told you, no. Look, we weren't much more than casual friends who enjoyed each other's company. We really didn't know each other that well."

"Do you know anything about his family background?"

"I know he was born in Lewis County. He told me his father's side of the family was from Corsica and his mother's side was originally from Watertown. That's it."

"Did he ever tell you why he bought that painting at your auction?"

"He wanted to support our lawsuit against the Resort."

"Did he tell you that?"

"Well, no I guess I just assumed it."

Did he ever tell you why he paid twelve hundred dollars for the painting?"

"I guess not. No, he never actually said why?"

"Did you and he ever go hiking together?"

"No, we talked about it a lot. But we never could find the time. I've been pretty busy."

"Where did you talk about hiking?"

"Lots of places. I do remember he said he loved the hike up Ampersand Mountain."

"Did you ever talk about hiking in the Tupper Lake area?"

"I don't remember. Maybe."

The interrogation continued for another hour. As they finished, Tony Goss went out of his way to be gracious. "I want to thank you again for coming in on such short notice. You were very generous with your time. I hope we didn't mess up your day too much."

"That's fine. I just hope you get this thing wrapped up."

Tommy Cook walked Alicia to the door while Reynolds and Goss went to Goss's office.

"Well Ed, what do we think, what do we know and what can we prove?"

"I think LaCroix and Benton may have worked together. At least, that's what I thought. I'm not so sure now. We don't know and can't prove a damn thing. How about you, what do you think?"

"My gut tells me she's involved somehow. But I must admit, she was cool today. What about Benton? You think we should wait before bringing him in?"

"You were right yesterday, let's not rush. You've got him under surveillance. Let's wait a few days and see if forensics comes up with anything else."

"Maybe LaCroix isn't involved at all," said Tommy Cook as he returned from escorting LaCroix to the front door. "Maybe she was just seeing the wrong guy at the wrong time."

"You might be right," Reynolds said.

"Then again, you might be wrong," Goss added.

THIRTY-ONE

THAT'S GOOD, that's very good."

Maureen McCalister had just read Shane Baxter's revised final summation. It was Wednesday morning. And, if needed, there was plenty of time left to make changes before Monday's hearing.

"I'm curious. Did you make many changes after reading *The Art of War*?"

"I completely rewrote it," Shane said. "The first version primarily focused on the strengths of our case. This new version starts with an emphasis on the weaknesses in the other side's case and concludes with the strengths of the Resort's case."

Maureen smiled, "Well, I'm not the judge, but if it were up to me, you win."

"Very nice of you to say, Maureen, but Ms. Bitch is a good lawyer. You haven't heard her side yet. Believe me when I say she'll be loaded for bear. Remember, she just got my motion to introduce new evidence two days ago. I doubt she was very happy when she listened to that tape."

"Hopefully the tape throws her off her game. Which is what it was meant to do. If she's focusing on how she can keep that out of the record, she's not focusing on final arguments."

"Don't underestimate her."

"My estimation is irrelevant. But I'm glad to see you aren't underestimating her. You're the one who's going to be on stage Monday. Do you expect this to go any differently than it would if . . . I mean, with Judge

Pennington presiding instead of Judge Kelly?"

"I think so. Kelly knew this stuff cold—all the evidence, all the briefs. If he were on the bench, I doubt he'd have many questions. Likely he'd have just let each side talk for an hour. With Judge Pennington only having a week to review the record, I think he'll interrupt us for clarification."

"Does he extend your time to make up for this?"

"Nope. Each side has one hour. That's it. I could get only two words out, and he can take up the rest of my time with questions."

Maureen was stunned. "Really? So all this work preparing final arguments could be a waste of time?"

"Welcome to Trial Lawyer 101, Mrs. McCalister."

"I was wondering why your summation wasn't a full hour. You were leaving time for questions."

"That's right. I've actually shortened it since Pennington took over. I'm sure Alicia has done the same thing."

"What about oral arguments for the new evidence motion?"

"I'm looking forward to that. Each side has only fifteen minutes. I'm guessing Hartman is going to let Ms. Bitch handle their side. She really has no legal basis to keep the evidence out. My guess is she'll argue irrelevance. She'll make a big deal how it has absolutely nothing to do with the case and doesn't belong in the record. It'll be a lot of style and little substance. Legal theater, if you will. But, as you learned at lunch last week, she's good at that. It'll be an Oscar-worthy performance. The good news is that legal theater seldom wins the day in court. The law usually wins, and the law is on our side. I think Pennington will rule in our favor"

"What's your argument to admit the evidence?"

"This entire case is about two things. First, the impact the Resort will have on the environment. They argue the development will 'threaten the ecological integrity and wild character' of the entire Adirondack Park. Our experts have thrown their arguments under the bus. I feel good about that part of the case."

"Second, we argue that Adirondack Environmental Watch opposes the development because they oppose *any* development in the Park. There is not one significant development project in the Park they have ever supported. Not one. This isn't about wise use, it's about no use. The 'no use doctrine' enshrined in the New York State Constitution as 'Forever Wild' has to do with state land, not private land. They want the APA to extend the 'Forever Wild' clause to the entire six million acres of the Park without legislative approval. The legislature makes policy and the APA is supposed to implement it. Essentially, Adirondack Environmental Watch is trying to bypass the legislature through regulatory fiat. They're doing it by pulling the APA's strings. Your recording of Ms. Bitch goes a long way toward proving that. The bottom line, your recording goes to the very heart of that second aspect of our case. Ms. Bitch's argument of irrelevance goes out the window. I am confident Pennington will find it admissible."

"The papers are saying one of our investors may have been involved in the disappearance of Judge Kelly. That worries me."

"I've been thinking a lot about that too," Shane admitted. "But remember, the papers are only saying Joseph Benton may have been involved. They don't connect him with the Resort. Right now, the only people that know he invested in the Resort are the state police and us. The state police are pretty good about information leaks. They run a tight ship. If Benton is involved in Kelly's disappearance, they probably plan on keeping his connection with the Resort quiet until his trial. That may be a year off. I really don't expect it will become public."

"I hope you're right."

"If it does become public, I'm prepared."

THIRTY-TWO

THE THURSDAY editorial in Saranac Lake's daily newspaper, *Adirondack News*, had nothing to do with the decision by Ed Reynolds and Tony Goss to have Joseph Benton arrested for murder. It was about the overwhelming evidence forensics had provided since the search of the Benton home. There was plenty they could now prove in court and the case was coming together. Nonetheless, the editorial was hard on the state police. They'd been quiet since Goss's brief statement to the media on Saturday. The newspaper had opined they should be doing a better job of keeping the public informed. Judge Kelly was a major public figure and the public had a right to know what was happening with the investigation, they argued.

While Goss seldom let editorials get to him, he knew the *Adirondack News* was arguing that the alleged "public right to know" trumped the goal of the state police to uncover evidence, find the guilty person, and have a rock-solid case for the district attorney to prosecute. Process versus results. Goss thought the public would prefer results.

The troopers arrived at the Benton Home at 11:27 a.m. on Thursday.

"What are you guys doing here? I hope you're bringing the stuff back you took on Saturday."

"Mr. Benton, please turn around and place your hands behind your back. You are under arrest for the murder of Judge Robert Kelly."

"What? Are you crazy? You're arresting me for the murder of that judge?"

"Turn around Mr. Benton, please." The troopers stepped inside the house. Their body language made it clear they were ready to use force if necessary. Joseph got the message. With the handcuffs in place, the trooper read Joseph his Miranda rights and asked if he understood.

"Yes, I understand. Where are you taking me?"

"We're going to Ray Brook. You'll be booked and arraigned, then transferred to Elizabethtown."

"Elizabethtown?"

"The Essex County Jail."

"I want to call my lawyer."

"Don't worry, you'll be given a chance to call him."

"What about my cat? Who's going to feed my cat?"

"Your lawyer can make those arrangements."

Joseph was placed in the back of the cruiser. Not a word was said during the trip to the Ray Brook, but Joseph was convinced that somehow, Jerry Doolin had something to do with his arrest.

Joseph quietly went through the fingerprinting, mug shots and DNA testing. After booking, he was escorted to the same interrogation room he had been in a few days earlier. Today, he was in handcuffs.

Tony Goss entered immediately and greeted Joseph. "Mr. Benton, you know why you're here?"

"Why are you charging me with murder?"

"Let's talk about that."

"I'm not going to talk to you about a damn thing. I want to talk to my lawyer."

Goss had hoped he would have a chance to ask Benton some questions, but as soon as a prisoner mentions the word lawyer, everything changes.

"Okay Mr. Benton, here's what we're going to do. You're going to have a chance to call your lawyer. In about two hours you will be arraigned, and then we'll have you transferred to Elizabethtown."

Joseph was escorted from the interrogation room and handed a telephone.

"I've been arrested. You need to get me out of here," he pleaded. I've been framed by a state trooper.

"Slow down, Joseph. What were you arrested for?" the attorney asked.

"Murder, they're saying I murdered that judge. I've been framed by a friend of mine who's a state trooper. You need to have him arrested. He's a thief and he's trying to steal my treasure. They're all working together. They're stealing hundreds of millions of dollars. You need to stop them."

"Joseph, stop. Now listen to me. Are you saying you have been arrested for the murder of a judge?"

"Yes! You have to get me out of here."

"Joseph, now listen to me carefully. Are you listening?"

"Yes."

"Don't talk to anyone. Do you understand?"

"I understand."

"You'll be going before a judge, probably in a few hours. You don't need me for that. The judge is going to explain the charges and your rights. Then he is going to ask you if you understand them. Just say yes. Not another word. Do you understand?"

"I understand."

"He then is going to ask you how you plead, just say not guilty and nothing else. Do you understand?"

"Yes, yes."

"If you've been arrested for murdering a judge you won't get bail. They're going to take you to the county jail. I'll be down there tomorrow and we can talk. Until then, don't say anything to anybody. Don't talk about being framed or stealing treasures. Don't say anything. Do you understand me?"

"Yes, I understand. I won't say anything. When can you get me out of here?"

"They have to give you a preliminary hearing next week. We'll ask the judge for bail then. We'll deal with this. Just remember Joseph, three words only, 'yes,' when asked if you understand the charges, and 'not guilty.' That's it. I'll see you tomorrow."

Smaller state police barracks like Ray Brook did not have holding cells, and Joseph was seated on a bench and handcuffed to an iron ring bolted to the wall while he waited for transportation. His heart was racing and he felt as though he was in some horrible dream.

THIRTY-THREE

BRENDAN MARTIN opened the doors to the courtroom at eight a.m. It was unusual for more than a handful of people to attend an administrative hearing. This morning there was a large crowd waiting and the room filled almost immediately. Fully half the people in the courtroom were media. Many of the press had been following this case for the full ten years. Many were there because the judge who had been slated to hear the case had been murdered. Others in the room were interested parties, mostly Tupper Lake people with property adjoining the Resort, business people, or members of the Town Council and Chamber of Commerce. For many, this was the end of a ten-year journey.

Maureen McCalister and two other Resort staff had front row seats just behind the defendants table.

Twelve APA staff members took up two rows of seats across the aisle, just behind the plaintiffs table. With them were four twenty-somethings, dressed for a day hike in the mountains. Ms. Bitch's staff, Maureen thought.

By eight thirty it was standing room only. Shane Baxter arrived and set his leather briefcase on the table. He took out two manila folders and a yellow legal pad and placed them neatly in front of him. Being left-handed, he placed his laptop on the table to his left.

The entire case record was on this computer. What amounted to over twenty-five thousand pages of transcripts, briefs and environmental studies.

As he opened to his index, Shane reminded himself that when this case started he was carrying his files around in banker's boxes. A backup laptop was in his car. Shane never came to court without a backup.

Dressed in his new camelhair sport coat, brown wool slacks, white shirt with button down collar and bow tie, Shane looked like an Adirondack lawyer. Sitting directly behind him, Maureen seemed confident.

Alicia LaCroix was dressed as if she'd walked out of a fashion magazine. She had her computer, but a stack of brown, accordion-type folders, each full of files, also stood on the table in front of her.

Sitting to the right of LaCroix was APA director, Richard Hartman. Hartman had just one manila folder and a legal pad. It was clear who was in charge.

It was three minutes to nine when Brendan Martin and the court reporter entered the courtroom taking their positions.

Judge Noah Pennington was a prompt man and at precisely nine a.m. he entered the courtroom. He was dressed in a business suit rather than the black robe traditionally seen in civil and criminal cases.

The bailiff was right on cue, "All rise. The administrative court for the State of New York is now in session. Judge Noah Pennington the third, presiding."

"Good morning everyone, please be seated."

"I see we have a large audience today. We welcome you to this proceeding. I would remind you this is a courtroom, and you will act accordingly. If there is any disruption of this hearing, I will clear the room."

"Before we get started, I would like to have a moment of silence for Judge Robert Kelly who presided over this case for almost ten years."

As he glanced up, Pennington saw that every head in the room was bowed. He was pleased there was no objection or interruption from any of the radical environmentalists. He had half expected it.

"Thank you. Before we get to final summation there is some business we need to deal with. Mr. Baxter, you have a motion to introduce new evidence. You have fifteen minutes. What say you?"

Other than the parties to the case, no one in the room was expecting anything other than final arguments. A murmur went through the crowd and Pennington quickly quieted the audience with his gavel.

"Good morning Judge. If it pleases the court, I believe our brief speaks for itself. Case law is clear and unequivocal. Attached as part of our brief, you have an affidavit from Mrs. McCalister attesting to the authenticity of this audiotape and the fact that it is introduced unedited. I could call on Ms. LaCroix to verify authenticity, but I don't expect her to question the tape itself, so I won't waste the court's time. If I have misjudged Ms. LaCroix, I do reserve the right to call on her during my rebuttal."

Shane returned to his seat. He was confident the law was on his side and thought keeping this part of the proceeding short would put him in the good graces of the judge.

"Ms. LaCroix, your response?"

"Thank you. Good morning Judge. I am a little disappointed Mr. Baxter didn't yield the balance of his time to me."

There was light laughter in the courtroom and again Pennington was quick with his gavel.

As Shane had predicted, LaCroix argued irrelevance. She spoke for the full fifteen minutes with little substance. The judge listened carefully, showing no emotion. At exactly fifteen minutes he interrupted, "Ms. LaCroix, your time is up. You have thirty seconds to wrap it up."

LaCroix finished and returned to her seat. The audience was confused, as the tape was never played in open court. A transcript and copy of the tape had accompanied the brief submitted by Baxter. Shane knew that if the judge allowed the evidence into the record, the press would have a field day once they got their hands on the transcript.

"Do you have any rebuttal Mr. Baxter?"

"No, Your Honor."

Pennington wasted no time. "My ruling is the new evidence will be allowed. Let's move on to final arguments. Ms. LaCroix and Mr. Hartman, you have one hour. How do you wish to split your time?"

"Thank you Your Honor. I am going to handle arguments for both Mr. Hartman and myself."

"You may proceed."

Alicia summarized her arguments with passion and clarity. The arguments were the same she had been making for years. "This project will fragment the great northern hardwood forests in the Park and foul its pure waters, the very foundation of the region's economy. Wildlife would be disturbed and very possibly never recover from this fragmentation." She pointed to the numerous environmental impact studies supporting her claims.

She went on to assert that the project's financing was "shaky at best," at a time of economic downturn. "Every real estate expert that has looked at this project agrees the Resort's projections are unreasonably optimistic."

As Alicia spoke, Maureen McCalister waited for her to claim "that the development would lead to massive global warming, earthquakes, volcanoes and asteroid strikes, resulting in the extinction of life on earth as we know it."

Trying not to repeat the mistake she had made earlier, Alicia finished her arguments in fifty-five minutes.

"Thank you Ms. LaCroix. Let's take a fifteen-minute recess before we hear from Mr. Baxter. We will start promptly at 10:35."

§

Shane began his summation by reviewing the testimony of the Resort's expert witnesses and exposing the weakness of Alicia's environmental impact studies. "This property has been regularly logged for almost a century, Your Honor. The fragmentation argument is nonsense. As is the clean water argument. Our wastewater treatment plant will employ the newest technology available." Shane went on, challenging every argument the opposition had presented.

He then acknowledged several issues where the plaintiffs had recommended changes to the development. "Plaintiffs have made this project better, Your Honor. For example, at their suggestion we have eliminated every structure from the ridgeline and upper elevations of Mount Morris. That is just one example. I won't waste the court's time by going through the seventeen other significant changes we have made at their suggestion. They are outlined in our brief so this court knows what they are. Your Honor, I do want to thank plaintiffs, on the record, for making this a better project."

Shane spent the balance of his time challenging the plaintiff's motives for the lawsuit. He reminded the court that Adirondack Environmental Watch had never supported a single development inside the Adirondack Park. He summarized the legislation creating the Adirondack Park Agency and the legislature's mandate to the agency. He reminded the court of ways in which that mandate had been abandoned.

Shane concluded with the enormous support the Resort enjoyed in the local community. "Tupper Lake needs this project to revitalize the local economy," he asserted. "More important, Your Honor, Tupper Lake wants this project."

To Shane's surprise, Judge Pennington did not interrupt him once. Shane completed his summation in just under forty-five minutes.

"Thank you Mr. Baxter. This court will be in recess until one p.m. I will issue my ruling then."

As the judge got up to leave the bailiff yelled, "All rise."

THIRTY-FOUR

JERRY HAD requested a two-week vacation. He needed the time to make sense of everything that had happened in the past week.

Joseph had been arrested four days ago and his preliminary hearing was scheduled for tomorrow, Tuesday afternoon. Jerry hadn't changed his mind about his friend's innocence. But he doubted the judge would grant him bail.

Every day since the arrest, Jerry had gone to Joseph's house to feed and water Bailey, and change her litter. Jerry didn't know what kind of cat Bailey was, but he did know that she liked him. Each time he walked in the door, she'd stroll up to him and would wind her way through his legs. After feeding her, he'd often stay and sit on the sofa. Bailey would join him and he would stroke her until she showed her appreciation by purring. He imagined Bailey missed her owner terribly. Jerry missed his friend and was worried about him. At these moments, Jerry would ponder what Joseph must be going through in jail. He had seen enough over the years to know it was not pleasant.

Today, while he was deep in thought, the phone rang. Jerry let the answering machine take the call. He noticed that Joseph had changed his message. Rather than giving his full name in the message, with an emphasis on the "Joseph," he had eliminated the name altogether.

The caller said, "Tim, this is Chris Westbrook over at The Ranger School. First, I wanted to tell you that I enjoyed our visit on Saturday."

Wrong number, Jerry thought, as he began to tune out the speakers words.

"Second, your secretary . . . I guess she is your secretary or your assistant . . . Alicia . . ."

This caught Jerry's attention.

"Anyway, she called and left a message yesterday asking the same questions about the shift in magnetic north. I assume you hadn't had a chance to tell her we discussed this on Saturday. I just tried to call her at the number she left and there was no answer. If you would, let her know I did try to reach her. There wasn't any machine so I thought I'd call you. I'll leave it in your hands. Call me if you have any more questions. So long."

Jerry just sat there, thinking. "What the hell . . . ? Who's Tim? No way Joseph would have told Alicia about the treasure. He certainly wouldn't have asked her do his research for him."

He realized Tim must be the phony name Joseph had used in the e-mails he sent out. Joseph had told him about that. But how would Alicia have found out? How would she have known to call The Ranger School?

"That's it!"

He called Tony Goss. "Tony, I've got it. I figured it out."

"Calm down, Jerry, what did you figure out?"

"Joseph Benton didn't kill Judge Kelly. I know who did. And I know why."

"Okay, what's your theory?"

Jerry first explained where he was, and why. He didn't want Goss to think he was freelancing on the case. "The call from The Ranger School just happened to come in while I was here feeding the cat. I couldn't help but hear it. Here it is, Tony. We know Joseph is a heavy drinker. He passes out almost every night. Once he's out, a bomb could go off in that house and Joseph wouldn't hear it. Alicia LaCroix may not have been a frequent visitor but she certainly was a regular visitor. At some point she sees Joseph enter his password and one night, after he passes out, she decides to troll his computer. She's a woman. She's nosy. I'm guessing your people found out everything about Joseph's family treasure in his files. I know he keeps a detailed journal. He used to write by hand in books. About ten years ago he switched to the computer.

"I'm guessing she saw his notes about the treasure. Joseph just recently figured out where it's buried. She's planning on stealing it. The lawsuit over the property is about to come to a conclusion and depending on the outcome, access to the property will be limited. LaCroix needed to make her move. She had to stop the hearing that was meant to happen last week. Maybe she went to see Kelly to try to get a postponement, and things got out of hand. I don't know. Something happens and she shoots the judge, maybe on purpose, maybe by accident. In any case, she needs to hang it on somebody, and who better than Joseph? She drives Kelly's SUV right into Joseph's driveway. He's passed out drunk, doesn't hear a thing. She drags the body down to the boat, binds his legs and hands with Joseph's tape. Gets some rope and a few cinder blocks and takes Kelly for a swim. She then drives Kelly's vehicle back to the hotel in Ray Brook. It's dark so nobody notices the hole in the windshield. She parks it behind the motel where she shot him, walks back across the road to the court where her car is parked, and drives home.

"Tony, I bet you didn't find Joseph's fingerprints on the adhesive of the duct tape. Did you?"

There was no response.

"Did you? Answer me."

"No, we didn't. There were unidentified fingerprints."

"She's a lawyer. Her fingerprints are on file. Not in the database, but they're on file with the New York State Bar Association. I'll bet you dinner, you'll get a match. Go talk to Joseph and ask him why he had LaCroix call The Ranger School. He'll think you're crazy because he didn't have LaCroix call. I'm the only person in the world he told about the treasure."

Tony had been listening intently. "We never did find a motive for Benton to kill the judge."

"Of course you didn't. Joseph had no motive to kill Judge Kelly. He had written permission to search the property. Win or lose the lawsuit, as long as those developers owned the property, he had permission from the owners. Hell, he was one of the owners. It's LaCroix who didn't have permission to be on that property. She's been trying to shut them down for ten years. The developers knew her and they would never give her permission to be there for any reason. She had a motive, a half billion dollars worth of motive."

"This is kind of reaching, Jerry."

"I'm not reaching at all, Tony. Nothing made sense to me until I heard that message. There was one small detail Joseph needed to locate the treasure," Jerry went on. "The folks at The Ranger School had the answers. Joseph just got the answers at the school on Saturday. If he was working with LaCroix he would have called her. He didn't. She was working alone.

"Why do you think she called you the other morning? She was fishing. She wanted to make sure you were going to arrest Joseph. She wanted to make sure she was in the clear. You told me you asked her why she thought Joseph would harm Judge Kelly. She said it probably had something to do with the Resort. Joseph never told her about his relationship with the Resort—his investment or the treasure. So, why would she have said that?"

"Check the prints on the tape, Tony."

"Doolin, you are either a genius or you are certifiably crazy."

"It's ironic . . . at the Resort offices they call her 'Ms. Bitch.' They have no idea."

"Jerry, I heard you were taking a few weeks off."

"That's right."

"As of seven a.m. tomorrow morning you're no longer on vacation. I want you in my office. We'll know by then if we have a fingerprint match. If we do, you and I have a busy day tomorrow."

"You got it."

Bailey had been sitting in a sunny spot on the floor. Jerry picked her up and stroked her. "If I'm right Miss Bailey, your daddy will be home in a few days. He can thank you for saving his ass. If it weren't for you, I wouldn't have been here to hear that message."

Bailey just went on purring.

THIRTY-FIVE

EVEN WITH lunch, the wait seemed like forever. At one o'clock exactly, the bailiff stood, "All rise."

When Judge Pennington took his seat, he spent a moment searching before he found his reading glasses. Then, for a time he stared out over his half glasses at the full courtroom, ignoring Hartman, LaCroix and Baxter. Anticipation filled the air. The silence was deafening.

Finally, the judge spoke. Slowly. Firmly. Deliberately.

"Oscar Wilde defined a cynic as one who knows the price of everything but the value of nothing. May the public be warned, the APA and Adirondack Environmental Watch seem to know the value of everything, but the price of nothing."

Judge Pennington then looked directly at Richard Hartman.

"Mr. Hartman, when it created the Adirondack Park Agency, the mandate from the New York State Legislature, enshrined in our State Constitution, was to keep public lands in the park 'Forever Wild.' During your tenure as APA director you've done a fine job with that. Thank you. In the case of private lands in the Park, the agency was charged with overseeing wise use.

"In 1892, Teddy Roosevelt declared the object of land policy was 'to consider how best to combine use with preservation.' Fine words. In fact, one could argue he got that philosophy directly from the New York State Constitution.

"I believe, Mr. Hartman, rather than combining wise use with preservation, you have been trying to ban use outright. So the question presents itself: Who will guard the guards? In regard to private land in the Adirondack Park, you have abandoned both your legislative and Constitutional mandate of traditional wise use philosophy in favor of the grab it all and lock it up philosophy of Ms. LaCroix there. Your position in the case at hand is a classic example of big government 'command and control' brand of environmentalism. That is not what the New York State Legislature intended and it's not what our Constitution mandates. It is now up to this court to guard the guards."

Judge Pennington turned to Alicia LaCroix, and with a look of controlled disgust went on. "Ms. LaCroix, there are legitimate disputes between *reasonable* people who want to use the forests for different purposes. You madam, are not reasonable. Sometimes, it seems, the Adirondacks are being loved to death by its friends. However, Ms. LaCroix, I don't believe you are even one of our friends. While sometimes misguided, at least our friends have good intentions."

"It appears that you, Ms. LaCroix, are the leader of a religious cult. You have your deity—the wilderness. You preach powers of salvation with a sense of 'renewal' that comes from a walk in the forest. You offer a sense of community with your day hikes, river runs and camping weekends. You offer an evangelical missionary program for the 'Great Unwashed' with your glossy literature. Your liturgical calendar even has a great 'holy day' that you will be celebrating in a few weeks while the rest of us celebrate Easter. Your holy day is called Earth Day. As the high priestess of the church of radical environmentalism in the Adirondacks, you are convinced of *your* moral and ethical superiority—no need for codes. That was evidenced by the audio tape introduced in court this morning. I suppose you can be forgiven. After all, one does not expect objective rational behavior from religious zealots, one expects devotion at the extreme.

"Radical environmentalists like you Ms. LaCroix, need the environment. The environment doesn't need environmentalists like you.

"Mr. Hartman and Ms. LaCroix, ideology, not reason, and certainly not the law, have been driving your behavior when it comes to the Adirondack Mountain & Lake Resort. That ends today. Here and now. My ruling is that the Adirondack Mountain & Lake Resort can immediately move forward with their development. The so called 'shovel ruling' is hereby overturned. Permits will be issued, construction can begin immediately. You will have my written ruling by the end of the week.

"Thank you. Court dismissed."

Already standing and without a moment's pause, almost as though it were pre-planned, the bailiff yelled, "All rise."

The judge had turned to leave the courtroom when Alicia LaCroix jumped out of her seat, "Judge, would the court entertain a motion to enjoin the ruling until appeals have been heard?"

The judge glanced at the bailiff who looked like he was trying to hold back a smile. He then turned to Alicia. "Ms. LaCroix, I said court dismissed. Now which of those two words are you having a problem with? If you want this court to entertain a motion to enjoin, send me a brief. Mr. Baxter can respond.

"Now Ms. LaCroix, Court Is Dismissed! Any part of that you don't understand?"

"No, Your Honor."

Shane turned around and leaned over the railing toward Maureen. "Congratulations Mrs. McCalister. And thank you for everything."

"And thank you," Maureen said. "Now, let's get back to the office and call corporate."

Maureen's smile said everything to Shane. For the first time since she had arrived in the Adirondacks, Maureen McCalister looked truly content.

THIRTY-SIX

BY SIX thirty a.m. Jerry Doolin was at the Ray Brook barracks reading the paper and waiting for Tony Goss. The ruling in the Resort case was the headline above the fold. Below the fold was a story about the preliminary hearing for Joseph Benton, scheduled for later in the day. Looking back to the Resort story, Jerry noticed a small side bar:

LaCroix Resigns

Sources report that Alicia LaCroix, executive director of Adirondack Environmental Watch, has resigned her position with the organization, effective immediately. LaCroix was unavailable for comment, but several people close to the organization have confirmed the departure. One board member, who asked not to be identified, said LaCroix has accepted a position as general counsel to the Washington offices of Environmental Watch. Adirondack Environmental Watch is one of two New York State affiliates of the Washington, DC, based organization.

Immediately following the dramatic loss in the Adirondack Mountain and Lake Resort case, Ms. LaCroix reportedly handed in her resignation. Leading environmentalists in the Adirondacks expressed disappointment. "Alicia LaCroix's departure is a great loss for the North Country and a great loss for the

environment," said William Dolan, director of Save the Wild.
"She will be missed."

Jerry had just finished reading the story when Goss arrived. "Have you seen this?" He handed Goss the folded newspaper.

Goss glanced at the story, "I'm not surprised. Her prints match the prints on the duct tape. We've had her under surveillance since midnight. Tommy Cook and Sam Perry are pulling together a team to pick her up. Want to join us?"

"Are you kidding?"

Two unmarked cars and one cruiser left Ray Brook at seven forty-five. At 8:03 they arrived at the LaCroix home. Another unmarked car was already there.

Alicia LaCroix had been awake for several hours, packing. The house and furniture were rented. Personal items were in boxes to be shipped and suitcases were by the front door to be put in the car. The car trunk was open with three bags already packed. As she opened the front door to take another bag to the car, she saw Goss, Cook and two other troopers she didn't recognize. The other two troopers had been sent to the rear of the residence.

She knew why they were there and immediately retreated into the house.

Without any warning, two pops came from the house with the sound of breaking glass. The four troopers were between their cars and the house with no protection. They recognized the sound and retreated back to their cars. Jerry Doolin felt a sting in his left arm. The uniformed trooper reached for the radio in his cruiser. "Shots fired, shots fired, need immediate backup."

The troopers at the back of the house had heard the shots and taken cover. Three more shots came from the front of the house. "Shit, this woman is crazy," Goss said. Tommy Cook took aim at the hole in the front window and fired three times.

After a short pause, four more shots came from the house. Sirens could be heard in the distance.

Jerry saw two neighbors open their front doors to see what the noise was. "Back in the house, back in the house," he yelled.

The troopers were just holding their position until backup arrived. SWAT would have been activated as soon as the "shots fired" call went in.

Goss noticed blood on the sleeve of Jerry's shirt. "You're hit. How bad is it?"

"Just a flesh wound. I'm fine."

Tony got on his radio again, "Officer hit. Need medical assistance."

Another sound of breaking glass came from the front window. This was different. There was no pop. "She threw the gun through the front window," Cook yelled.

"I'm coming out," Alicia yelled. "Don't shoot."

The front door opened. "Stop and turn around, face the door," Cook yelled. "Let me see your hands." As soon as Cook saw her hands were empty he yelled again, "put your hands behind your head." LaCroix was turning around. "I said put your hands behind your head."

Everybody had maintained their positions behind their cars with their guns pointed at LaCroix.

"Take three steps backward."

LaCroix took the three steps.

"Keep your hands behind your head and get on your knees."

Still behind their cars, the troopers were now standing. Cook could see the troopers who had been at the rear were now on each side of the house, their guns drawn.

LaCroix was on her knees. "Lie face down, and keep your hands behind your head."

Four more cruisers had arrived. Still more sirens could be heard in the distance.

Goss and Cook were approaching slowly, ready in case LaCroix tried to make a move. Her gun was on the porch about fifteen feet from where she laid.

The other uniformed trooper went to check on Doolin. Jerry's sleeve was soaked with blood. He could see an ambulance down the road being held up by a cruiser until they were sure it was safe.

Tommy Cook walked up the four steps to where LaCroix was lying. "Don't make one move lady." His gun was holstered and handcuffs were in his hand. Three guns were still pointed at LaCroix.

With a knee in her back, Cook placed the cuffs. He was not gentle.

The trooper with Jerry Doolin motioned for the ambulance. Neighbors were looking through their windows or gawking from their front porches.

Goss went to check on Jerry. The ambulance was just pulling up. He took one glance at Jerry's arm, "Look, you candy ass, if you wanted a vacation that bad, you could have just told me. You didn't have to get yourself shot. Go get that fixed. I'm looking forward to a little conversation with Ms. Bitch. I'll see you a bit later."

Jerry was placed in the ambulance and taken to the Adirondack Medical Center less than a mile away.

LaCroix was placed in the back of one of the cruisers and taken to the Ray Brook barracks.

Goss asked Tommy Cook to stay and supervise the investigation of her house and car. He was anxious to talk with Alicia LaCroix. As he drove away he saw the "vultures" from the press arriving.

Back in the barracks, Goss checked to see if Alicia had been processed. "Were there any problems with Miranda?"

"None," was the response. Goss requested that she be escorted to the interrogation room. Then he called Ed Reynolds. "Ed, what time is the Joseph Benton hearing this afternoon?"

"Four o'clock. Why?"

Goss explained what had happened. "I'm going to talk to her now. I'll call you later."

"Tony, she's a lawyer. There's no way she's going to talk to you."

"I'm not so sure Ed. She said something about wanting to talk. I think she wants a deal."

"Tell her if she cooperates with you, I'm willing to listen. If she doesn't, I won't even talk to her about a deal. Call me at three."

Goss hung up and looked at his watch. Five hours. He entered the interrogation room and just stared at LaCroix. He knew how much trouble this woman was in, yet he was still taken aback by her stunning looks. She was wearing tight jeans and a low cut red blouse. Her blond hair looked unwashed. Her wrists were now cuffed in front and her well-manicured hands were folded on the table.

"We meet again Ms. LaCroix."

Alicia said nothing.

"I'm told you said something about wanting to talk. Did you change your mind?"

There was silence. Goss let the moment last. He knew the one who spoke next, lost. The silence continued.

"Here's what I want," LaCroix said finally. "Before I say a word, I want a commitment from the district attorney that he won't ask for the death penalty."

"Interesting you bring up the district attorney, Ms. LaCroix. I just got off the phone with him. Here's what he said to tell you. If you cooperate with me now, he's willing to listen to what you have to say. If you don't cooperate with me, he won't even talk to you about a deal."

Again, silence.

Goss decided to add a little incentive. "You might be interested to know that your fingerprints were found on the duct tape binding Judge Kelly's hands and legs. I think there were seven different prints of yours they found."

More silence.

"You think about that for a minute, Ms. LaCroix. I need a cup of coffee." He left the room.

For thirty minutes, he let Alicia ponder her situation.

When Goss reentered the room, LaCroix began to talk. And, talk she did. For the next three hours she explained how she had found out about the treasure by trolling through Joseph Benton's computer. She had even found his family bible.

She told Goss how she tried to convince Judge Kelly to postpone the hearing for sixty days so that she could access the property. The only people watching the property were her employees, and she could fix that. He refused. It was supposed to be an off-the-record conversation with Kelly, after office hours. When he told her he had to notify the defense of the conversation, she shot him. She told how easy it had been to lay the murder at the feet of Joseph Benton. She had discovered he had two million dollars invested in the Resort, and she knew that information would come out in any investigation. He was the perfect foil. She used his boat, rope, duct tape and cinder blocks. All the evidence would point to him. It was the perfect crime.

"There is no such thing as the perfect crime, Ms. LaCroix."

"Tell Ed Reynolds I will plead guilty, if he agrees to my terms."

"I'll tell him."

The entire confession was on video tape, including LaCroix waiving her rights to remain silent and her rights to have a lawyer present. She was asked several times during her statement if she wanted a lawyer present. Each time she refused.

It was after three when Goss made the call to Ed Reynolds. Reynolds was in Elizabethtown ready for the Benton preliminary hearing. He told Reynolds he had never seen such a comprehensive confession. Everything she said cleared Joseph Benton completely. Reynolds was pleasantly surprised at the news.

"I'll take care of everything here Tony. Benton will be ready for the ride back to Cranberry Lake by four thirty."

"I'll have a car there for him."

THIRTY-SEVEN

THE PRELIMINARY hearing started at four p.m. Joseph was brought into the courtroom along with seven other prisoners and seated in the front row where the public would normally sit. Further back were about a dozen members of the media. He saw his attorney sitting at the front table on the right side of the aisle. When he met with him yesterday, his lawyer had warned him the possibility of bail was slim.

"All rise," came the voice as the judge entered the courtroom.

"What's our first case today?"

"The State of New York verses Joseph B. Benton."

Joseph's lawyer stood and turned, looking for Joseph. He motioned him to the table. As Joseph approached he rose and whispered, "Everything's fine, Joseph. Don't worry." He motioned to Joseph to stand beside him as Ed Reynolds started to talk.

"Your Honor, the state is requesting that all charges against Mr. Benton be dropped. This morning, the person responsible for this crime was apprehended and made a full confession. The state would also like to apologize to Mr. Benton, on the record, for any inconvenience we have caused him."

The judge responded, "Okay Mr. Benton, all charges against you are hereby dismissed. You're free to go."

In unison, a dazed Joseph and his attorney thanked the judge. Joseph looked at his lawyer, "What just happened?

The lawyer whispered to Joseph, "Court is still in session. Let's go outside."

In the hallway, his lawyer told Joseph that Alicia LaCroix had confessed to the Kelly murder and her attempt to frame him. Joseph was stunned.

"Why did she do it?"

"I don't know the details. But I understand you have a ride waiting outside to take you home. It's highly unusual, but apparently Ray Brook has arranged transportation for you."

A state police cruiser was waiting in front of the building. A trooper was standing by the open rear door. "Mr. Benton?"

"I'm Joseph Benton."

"My orders are to escort you to Saranac Lake."

"No handcuffs?"

"No sir, just a pleasant ride to Saranac Lake."

"Well, let's go."

Joseph thanked his lawyer and climbed into the back seat. He strapped his seatbelt and settled in for the forty-five minute ride. As they entered Saranac Lake, the trooper pulled into the McDonalds parking lot, took out his cell phone and punched some numbers.

"Trooper Pertowski here. ETA is five minutes." There was a short pause. "Yes, Sir."

He placed the phone on the seat next to him.

Another mile and they were turning right onto Main Street, then left onto Broadway.

"Where are we going?"

"My orders are to take you to the Adirondack Medical Center. Senior Investigator Goss will meet you there."

"Why are we going to the hospital? There's nothing wrong with me."

"Those are my orders."

Joseph wanted to go home. He was worried about Bailey and he was tired and confused. "What's going on now?" he groaned.

Tony Goss met the car as it pulled up to the main entrance of the hospital.

"Mr. Benton. I'm glad you could meet me here."

"Did I have a choice?"

"No, I guess you didn't, did you? Please, let's go inside where we can talk."

Joseph shrugged and followed Goss into the hospital, past the large reception and waiting area. They then turned right toward the emergency room. Goss led him into a small conference room where doctors meet with families of ER patients.

"Have a seat, Mr. Benton."

Joseph was frustrated. "Can you please tell me what this is about?"

"First of all, I want to apologize for everything we put you through this past week. Second, I thought you should know what a lucky man you are."

"What are you talking about?"

"Just down the hall is a friend of yours, Jerry Doolin. Jerry was shot this morning in the process of apprehending Alicia LaCroix. It's not serious, he's fine. I know what you said the other day about him wanting to steal from you. I thought you should know, he never gave up on you. Throughout the entire investigation he kept telling me you were innocent. Before we searched your home that night he tried to resign from his twenty-two-year career because he couldn't bear to participate in what was about to happen to you. He didn't want to help with the search. I talked him out of resigning. I told him if he really wanted to help you, he should play devil's advocate for me. He did. But of course, he couldn't tell you what he was doing."

Joseph shook his head, still puzzled.

"Mr. Benton, all the evidence pointed directly to you. Ms. LaCroix did a masterful job with her frame up. It was your boat, your tape, your rope, your cinder blocks. Everything told us it was you, except your friend Jerry."

"My friend Jerry."

"Yesterday afternoon, he called me from your home. He's been there every day taking care of your cat. He was the one who figured out Alicia LaCroix murdered the judge. I had to confirm a few things, but he was absolutely right. We picked her up this morning. She was a little uncooperative. She fired a few shots."

"What are you telling me?"

"Jerry took one in his arm."

"No way!"

"He'll be sore and out of work for a month or two, but he'll be fine. The bullet went right through some muscle. He was lucky it didn't hit the bone."

Joseph was silent. Tony thought he saw a tear forming in Joseph's eye.

"We have a little problem I was hoping you could help us with."

"What's that," Joseph asked.

"Your buddy in there is all groggy with the morphine they've been giving him for pain. Still, he's been a pain in the ass all afternoon, and the hospital staff doesn't want to keep him overnight. I was wondering if you wouldn't mind giving him a ride home? We had his car brought over from Ray Brook."

Joseph wiped something from his eye and looked at Goss. "If he's being such a pain in the ass, maybe we should let him walk to Cranberry Lake."

"We could do that. After all, he was shot in the arm, not the leg."

They both smiled. "Can I see him?"

"I didn't tell him we were bringing you here. He's going to be surprised."

Lying in his bed in a curtained cubical, Jerry heard a familiar voice talking to a nurse.

"Miss, I'm with the Ajax Wig Emporium, I was wondering if you had any bald patients here today I could talk with?"

The nurse just smiled and tilted her head toward Jerry's cubicle.

"Joe Boy, is that you?"

The curtain was pulled back, "The name is Joseph."

Goss peeked his head around the corner, "It looks like you're in good hands Jerry, I'm going to leave."

Jerry pointed to Joseph, "Tony, is this your doing?"

"I'm just trying to save the taxpayers' money. I figured it was cheaper if Joseph drove you home."

THIRTY-EIGHT

JERRY AND Joseph went to Judge Kelly's funeral together and discretely took seats in the back of the crowded church. Judge Noah Pennington gave an emotional eulogy that was interspersed with several humorous personal stories. The service was more a celebration of Judge Kelly's life than a mourning of his passing. As they were leaving, they ran into Tony Goss.

Tony asked if everything had been returned in proper order. Joseph told him the seven banker's boxes and two computers had been returned several days earlier.

"Everything appears to be in order. Thanks for getting these things back as quickly as you did." He understood that for now they had to keep the boat and other items as evidence.

Driving through Tupper Lake, Joseph took Jerry to the Big Tupper Ski Area and showed him the place near the golf course where he had been searching. He then drove up the road to the area he planned to search tomorrow. "I hope you're going to join me?"

"My arm's still a little sore, but you couldn't keep me away."

Joseph's new Minelab E-Trac metal detector had arrived three days ago and he was excited. For years he had used a Minelab Explorer II as his primary detector. He told Jerry that while he loved the Explorer, the new E-Trac had a number of high-tech features. Metal detection technology had advanced a great deal over the years. The biggest change was computerization. The E-Trac allowed Joseph to download settings and discrimination patterns via a USB port. Joseph was also interested in the E-Trac's greater detection depth, higher sensitivity over a wide range of targets, and more accurate identification of target characteristics.

Ever since the gadget had arrived, Joseph had been "field testing" it in his yard. He was eager to use it on the Resort property.

Several years earlier Joseph had spent a great deal of money on a Pulse Star II Pro, which he'd never had a chance to use because it required two people to carry. He was looking forward to trying it out with Jerry's help. Jerry laughed and called the metal detectors "Joey's toys." His friend corrected him, "Joseph's toys."

The two had spent a great deal of time over the past two weeks talking about the events that almost destroyed their friendship. Joseph had apologized a hundred times for thinking Jerry had betrayed him. Now, on the drive from Tupper to Cranberry Lake, Joseph started to apologize again. Finally, Jerry had to put an end to it. "If you apologize one more time, I'm going to shoot you, shave your head and feed you to the fish, not necessarily in that order."

Over the past several weeks Joseph had continued his research. He described to Jerry the conversation with Chris Westbrook, the director at The Ranger School. Westbrook had told Joseph that the hills west of the Adirondack's contained a fair amount of limestone and therefore had natural caves. He also warned him there were a few areas of high iron content that would often interfere with magnetic compasses.

Joseph had thought the Adirondack Mountains were part of the Appalachian Range. Westbrook told him he was wrong, "The Adirondacks were part of the Canadian Shield."

"The geology within the Park itself is primarily granite underneath clay soil and sand deposits left by the glaciers," Joseph told Jerry. "There are very few natural caves."

Jerry thought about this for a moment. "So you're saying at Big Tupper we'll be looking for a man-made cave?"

"Exactly, Westbrook told me if the treasure is in this part of the Park, they would have to blast the rock to make a cave."

Joseph had been searching near the golf course at the base of Mt. Morris, to the left of the entrance to the ski area. Now that Westbrook had done the math, he knew the correct heading was more than a half mile away on the right side of the access road to the ski area.

The two friends tried to imagine Joseph's famous ancestor planning and executing the entire process of hiding treasure. "He must have hired surveyors to pinpoint the location without telling them why he was interested. Maybe he told them he was thinking of buying the property," Joseph speculated.

"Transporting the treasure must have been really difficult," Jerry added. "It would have been heavy."

"Family legend says when he originally arrived at Lake Bonaparte, the wagons he brought were each drawn by six horses. In 1830, the road, if you could call it that, from Lake Bonaparte to the Raquette River would have been rugged at best. More like a trail." Joseph went on, "Any rain at all, while the treasure was being transported, would have caused enormous problems. The wagons would have gotten stuck in the mud."

"Maybe they moved the treasure in the winter, when the ground was frozen," Jerry suggested. "If the ice was thick enough, they could have taken it right up the Raquette River, over Raquette Pond, directly to the base of Mt. Morris."

"He must have really trusted the servants who helped him move the stuff," Joseph mused. "I wonder if any of them returned to the hiding place to steal it." The thought disturbed him.

"The king would have taken these servants with him back to France. They wouldn't have had the resources to return to America on their own," Jerry reassured him.

Joseph planned to take all three metal detectors with him. Jerry's arm was still sore, so he couldn't handle a unit himself.

"You can carry one end of the Pulse Star," Joseph told him.

"I'm keeping track of my time and plan on sending you a bill," Jerry joked.

"Actually, I was planning on sending you a bill, baldy."

"You send me a bill. Why?"

"This is all part of your rehab for that arm."

"Send it to my insurance company. I'm sure they'll be happy to pay."

As Joseph dropped Jerry at his house, they agreed to meet at six a.m.

As he was walking away from the car, Jerry turned and said, "Joe Joe, tomorrow you may be a half a billion dollars richer, and I'll still be a public servant."

"Don't count my chickens before they're hatched, baldy." He turned onto Colombian Road and yelled out the window as he drove away, "By the way, the name is Joseph."

THIRTY-NINE

THE EQUIPMENT was sitting in the driveway at five thirty a.m. waiting for Jerry and his pickup. It wasn't often Joseph was awake this early. Until recently, it was even less frequent he woke up without a hangover. Joseph had been shocked at everything that had taken place at his home while he had been in a drunken stupor. He had asked Jerry for advice. Pleased at his interest in getting help, Jerry had taken Joseph to an AA meeting in Star Lake. One day at a time, Joseph was staying sober.

Jerry arrived at 6:05 in his well-dented white truck, circa 1978. Several years earlier he had bought the truck as a second vehicle to help with chores. It was old and beat up, but reliable. Jerry actually enjoyed working on it and keeping it running. In the Adirondacks, a pickup can be quite useful. However, he'd discovered that with a pickup you tend to acquire a lot of new friends—friends who don't have a pickup.

The three metal detectors and several shovels were placed in the bed of the truck. He'd also included a large blue tarp in case they found something and needed to cover it for the ride home. Both men had backpacks as well, with water bottles and energy bars.

On the drive to Tupper Lake, Joseph told Jerry he was glad it was a cloudy day. "Easier to see the LED readout on the metal detectors," he explained.

Jerry asked Joseph how he went about covering an area. The response is what he had expected. It was a random search at best.

"Let me tell you how the state police do it."

Jerry went on to explain how they set up a grid system and methodically worked each grid. "It's like what archeologists do," he said. "Lucky for you I brought stakes and plenty of line. We can set up our own grid and cover the area methodically. I don't know what you would do without me."

"I'm not an idiot, why do you think I brought you along? I knew even without your arm you might be useful."

Jerry suggested that, before laying out the grid, they just walk the area. "We can get the lay of the land and even though it has been 180 years since the treasure was buried, maybe we'll get lucky we'll see some kind of anomaly in the terrain where a cave might have been created."

As they crossed the Raquette River Joseph looked at the ski area. The sun was just coming up and they could see that there was still snow on the trails. To Joseph, it was a beautiful sight and he was excited this day had finally arrived. They stopped for breakfast at the diner in Tupper Lake where they took a booth near the back and spread out a map. "We'll start just below that point," Joseph suggested, pointing to the northern border of the Resort property line, just south of a portion of the golf course. There was a fairly sharp one-hundred-fifty-foot rise in elevation to their south. "A good place to carve a cave," Jerry said. Both men were getting excited.

They parked on the access road to the Big Tupper Ski area, just above the golf course. It was still a quarter mile walk to their target area. In the woods there were a few areas of snow. It would be another five or six weeks before the leaves would be on the trees. "This is the perfect time to search this area," Joseph thought. They were only a hundred feet from the clearing they had targeted when Jerry pointed to something he thought was unusual. Joseph walked up to the area and found the remnants of an old foundation. "Not what we're looking for, but good eye."

While the area was heavily forested with a combination of hardwood trees and pines, they kept reminding themselves that the treasure had been buried 180 years ago. This place would have looked very different then. To the south, between them and Route 30, there were a number of privately owned properties. Between Route 30 and the lake, there was only a few hundred feet of land, although Joseph told himself that in 1830 there would have been much more. When Setting Pole Dam and Pierce-field Dam were built, the level of the lake would have risen significantly. The possibility certainly existed that the treasure was now under water.

Joseph and Jerry had talked about this on the drive over from Cranberry Lake. They tried to think like King Joseph. They figured if Bonaparte had gone to this much trouble to hide the treasure, he would have made the final effort to go up the mountain, at least a little way. They still figured their best bet was the area they were now searching. For another two hours the two men walked the target area.

"Over here." Again, it was Jerry who had noticed something unusual. Just above a grassy clearing, he noticed a bulge in the hill. This was unlike anything they had seen in the other areas they had looked. Joseph walked around the area. Why would the slope have a large bulge in that one area? "It may be a chunk of granite just under the surface," Joseph suggested. "It's definitely something to look at once we get the equipment out."

"It could also be debris from digging a cave," Jerry suggested.

"Maybe," Joseph agreed.

They continued up the hill without noticing anything unusual, but both men wondered why the clearing was there. "Maybe there was a house here at one point," Joseph suggested. "With the equipment, I might be able to locate a foundation under the soil."

They were close to the sharp 150 foot rise, and the terrain was getting quite steep. Jerry looked around and said, "If I were going to hide a treasure this is where I'd dig a cave. Let's get the equipment."

Back at the truck, Joseph grabbed the Minelab E-Trac while Jerry grabbed the large roll of twine, a hammer and a bag of stakes. Setting up a grid in the woods would be a challenge, he thought to himself. There was still a good chill in the air at the end of March.

Jerry went to the cab and got out Joseph's maps. He wanted to take another look now that they had walked the property. With a bottle of water and an energy bar, he sat on the open bed of the pickup studying the topographical map and a copy of the medallion from King Joseph's bible.

"Joseph, look at this." He pointed to the area they had been walking. "See this hill? It's almost due north of the ski trails. We were here, just the other side of it. Now look at the medallion. These two points could be the top of that hill and the top of Mt. Morris. That line could be the shoreline of the lake before the dams were built. We were just walking right where the 'X' is."

Joseph stared at the medallion and the map. "X marks the spot! Let's go."

"Slow down cowboy, let me finish my water. You should have some too. Even though it's chilly you still need to keep hydrated."

While Joseph drank, Jerry transferred all the water and energy bars to one backpack. The other he filled with the stakes, twine and hammer and put the packs on the ground with the Minelab E-Track and two shovels. Just then another pickup pulled up behind them and parked.

"Can I help you guys?" the stranger asked.

Jerry and Joseph weren't quite sure what to say. Joseph spoke up, "We're fine. Just doing a little metal detecting."

"This is private property. We don't allow visitors. I'm sorry, but you'll have to leave."

"I have permission to be here," Joseph said.

"Permission from who?"

Joseph didn't want to say he was an investor, "From the owners of the property."

"I work for the owners, and I don't know anything about anybody having permission to be here. Who did you talk to?"

"I have permission from the owners in New York."

"This property is managed by our offices here in Tupper Lake. I doubt very much the folks in New York would be giving anybody permission to be digging holes here." He nodded toward the shovels. "I'm afraid you'll have to pack up and leave. Otherwise, I'll have to call the state police."

"I am the state police." Jerry took out his wallet and showed the man his badge and identification. "Jerry Doolin," he stuck out his hand. "And, this is Joseph Benton."

"Good to meet you, I'm Craig Werner. I work for the Resort people. With all due respect, this is still private property and you can't be here."

"Joseph does have permission to be here. If you want, we can go back to your offices and verify that with Mrs. McCalister." Jerry thought dropping Maureen's name would end the discussion.

"You know Mrs. McCalister?" the man asked.

"I met her last week, along with Shane Baxter. How is she settling in to her new surroundings?"

"Just fine, the court decision the other day certainly took the pressure off."

"I bet it did. Tell her and Mr. Baxter, congratulations for me."

"I will. I still need to confirm that you have permission to be here."

Jerry could see that Joseph was getting irritated. Jerry was getting a bit frustrated himself. "Let's take a ride over to the office and get this straightened out. Shall we?"

They loaded their gear back into the pickup and followed Werner to the Resort offices.

FORTY

THE MOOD at the Resort offices was quite different than when Jerry had last been there. Two weeks ago, the final hearing in the court case, as well as the missing judge, were hanging heavy. Today, a feeling of relaxed excitement was in the air. There also seemed to be much more activity.

Young Tommy was at the reception desk. "Can I help you?"

"We met two weeks ago. I'm Jerry Doolin from the state police."

"Sergeant Doolin, I didn't recognize you without your uniform. I'm Tommy. Good to see you again. Are you here to buy a house in our new resort?"

Jerry laughed, "No, Tommy, sorry. This is Joseph Benton. He's one of the investors in the Resort."

"Mr. Benton, it's a pleasure to meet you."

In the background, Craig Werner had a sinking feeling in his stomach. These two men hadn't told him Benton was one of the investors.

Joseph put out his hand, "How do you do, Tommy."

"Is Maureen in?" Jerry asked.

"She sure is. Let me tell her you're here."

Tommy disappeared down the hall.

"Sergeant Doolin, my Irish friend. Welcome back. I read about your heroics in the paper. How is your arm?"

"Doing well, thank you, but today it's just Jerry. I'm off duty. And there were no heroics involved. I was in the wrong place at the wrong time. I forgot to duck. I want you to meet a friend of mine, Joseph Benton. Joseph is one of your investors. He lives in Cranberry Lake."

"Mr. Benton. It's so nice to meet you. I've read a lot about you too in the past few weeks. I've been very concerned that your investment in the Resort has caused you so much trouble."

"I'm not Mr. Benton. That was my father. Please call me Joseph."

"What brings a state trooper and one of our investors here today? I hope you don't want your money back."

Everybody laughed.

Craig Werner spoke up and explained what had happened. He turned to Joseph, "Mr. Benton, I'm so sorry, I had no idea you were an investor in the Resort. If I had known, I would never have made you come over here."

"You were just doing your job. And doing it well, I might add. I wanted to meet Maureen anyway."

The compliment in front of his boss made Craig feel much better. Maureen thanked Craig and invited her two guests into her office.

Nothing about the treasure or Joseph's heritage had come out in the press, so Joseph simply explained that metal detecting was a hobby of his and, when he invested in the Resort, he'd obtained written permission to use his metal detector on the site. "I thought I'd go over the property before you began construction. And since my bald-headed friend was taking a few weeks off, I brought him along for some exercise and fresh air. I apologize for any trouble I've caused. We should have stopped here first to let you know we'd be on the property."

"No apology needed. What do you think you'll find?"

"Usually we just end up finding old buttons, sometimes old coins, that kind of stuff. More than anything, it's a great way to get exercise."

"It sounds quite interesting. Do you have a copy of the written permission we gave you? I'd just like to have a copy in my files for the insurance company. In case of an accident or something. It would also be a good idea to have a copy on file in case you're stopped in the future and I'm not here."

"It's at home. I normally don't carry that kind of thing with me."

"Why would you?" Maureen smiled.

"I'll be glad to e-mail you a copy tomorrow."

"Never mind. I can get a copy from our corporate office in New York." Maureen looked at her watch, "Can I buy you two gentleman lunch?"

"Thanks for the offer," Joseph said. "But we need to get back to the woods. Maybe another time."

"Another time it is. I apologize for the interruption. Happy hunting."

"Thanks. And no apology needed. I should have stopped by to let you know what we were doing."

Back in the pickup, Jerry expressed his frustration at the delay, but Joseph was calm. "I've been at this thirty years, buddy. An hour's delay isn't the end of the world."

They parked in the same spot they had earlier, grabbed their gear and headed into the woods.

"How's your arm doing buddy?"

"A little sore. But I'll make it."

"Good, I'd hate to leave you in the woods. Worst case scenario, we've got shovels. I could just bury you right here."

While walking to the clearing they agreed that Jerry would begin to set up a grid system, while Joseph set up the metal detector with the proper combination of settings for the local conditions. He had also brought his headphones to extend the battery life of the equipment.

The detector was set to alert only on non-ferrous targets. He was look-ing for gold and silver and didn't want hits on iron as someone searching for civil war or World War II relics would.

While Jerry laid out the grid, Joseph headed up the hill to the anomaly they had spotted earlier. He thought this would be a good place to test his equipment. Joseph climbed above the bulge in the landscape and turned on the metal detector. He had not even plugged in the headset when a loud, high-pitched tone pierced the forest air. The tone indicated an extremely strong hit. Joseph was sure something was wrong. He needed to adjust his settings. These kinds of false hits were common when first turning on a metal detector. This was the new unit he had only tried in his backyard. He turned down the volume and placed the headset over his ears. Looking at the readout, he adjusted his settings. The sound continued. More adjustments. He still couldn't get the irritating noise to go away. "What am I doing wrong?" he asked himself. "Maybe I should have brought the Explorer." The other unit was a simpler device and Joseph was much more familiar with its operation.

As he started to walk back toward Jerry and the clearing, the sound went away. The readouts indicated nothing was there. Joseph was baffled. Just one more setback, he thought.

Then it hit him. "It couldn't be."

He turned around and walked back up the hill. As soon as he approached the anomalous bulge, the detector started to scream again. He walked around the area and every time he moved away from the anomaly, the tone in his ears went away. As he came closer, the tone returned. The tone was stronger when he stood in front of the bulge and pointed the metal detector at almost a ninety degree angle toward the hill. "Could this be it?" He called Jerry.

"Bring the shovels," he yelled. "I found something."

He was several hundred yards from where Jerry was building his grid, and Jerry didn't hear him. Joseph set the metal detector down and walked back to the clearing. As he got closer he called again and Jerry looked up.

"I thought you got yourself lost. Where have you been?"

"Testing my equipment. I think I found something . . . something big. Let's get the shovels."

At the bulge Joseph turned on his metal detector and unplugged the headphones. The loud tone filled the forest.

"Wow," Jerry thought. "And you don't get that when you walk away?"

"Nope."

"Let's start digging," Jerry said.

"I'll dig. You don't need to do any more damage to that arm." He pointed to a rock. "Have a seat over there."

Joseph had an odd feeling. After thirty years of searching, he had a shovel in his hand and might be on the verge of finding his family heritage. "King Joseph may have been right here 180 years ago," he said. Jerry could see the emotion in his friend's eyes as Joseph studied the bulge in the hill. He wasn't quite sure where to begin. "Should I start on the top or here at the base?" he asked.

"It's your treasure buddy. Start wherever you want."

Joseph started in the middle of the bulge. He removed over eight inches of top soil before he started to hit rock.

Joseph was taking a break as he and Jerry discussed what they were looking at. After two hours of digging, Joseph had cleared an area about five foot square. It was obvious this was a manmade site. Under the cleared topsoil lay a pile of smallish rocks of various sizes, none larger than eighteen inches in diameter.

Jerry was getting bored just watching, "Joe Boy, why don't you move to the top of the pile and clear the dirt while I start rolling some of these rocks out?"

"I don't want you to hurt yourself. And, the name is Joseph."

"Don't worry. I can use one hand and let them roll down the hill."

The two worked another three hours. The sun was low in the sky and it was beginning to get cold.

"Let's call it a day," Joseph suggested. I'm coming back tomorrow. You're welcome to join me."

"I told you before, I wouldn't miss this for the world."

Before leaving the site, they stepped back and looked at their work. "I think the king would have had more help," Joseph commented. "One damaged state trooper who can't even remember my name is kind of pathetic." He put his hand on Jerry's shoulder. "But, I am glad you're here."

"Thanks buddy. I'll take that as a compliment."

On the drive back to Cranberry Lake they talked about how much easier it would be with heavy equipment, but they agreed they couldn't get anyone else involved. And Joseph's permission didn't include bringing earth-moving machines onto the property.

Tomorrow they would bring a wheelbarrow.

FORTY-ONE

THEY WERE at the site by seven fifteen. They had a feeling that they were digging at exactly the same spot King Joseph Bonaparte had dug, 180 years ago. Privately, Joseph thought he'd felt the presence of his ancestor while digging yesterday.

"How's your arm today?" he asked Jerry.

"Good. I was a little worried I overdid it yesterday, but it's fine."

They'd used the wheelbarrow to carry the shovels and a pick to the site. Working side by side, the two men rolled rocks down the hill. After several hours of work, Jerry noticed that many of the rocks now looked different than those he'd seen earlier.

"Joey, look at this." He showed a rock to his friend. "This looks like scorch marks, maybe from blasting. Dynamite in the 1830's had much more black powder than today."

"The name is Joseph. Do you really think scorch marks would last 180 years?"

"They could. We may be getting close. Scorch marks would be on the rocks closest to the entrance of a cave they may have blasted back then."

They kept digging. Within minutes, near the top of what had been the bulge on the hillside, they hit solid rock. They were forced to focus their efforts below the solid area. Jerry was using both hands at this point. Suddenly Jerry put his hand on Joseph's back and whispered, "Stop." He paused for a moment. "Listen."

They both heard the sound of footsteps in the woods. From the direction of the clearing, they saw Craig Werner heading their way.

"Good morning gents."

"Good morning Craig," they said in unison.

"I was doing my rounds and saw your truck. Thought I'd see how you're doing. Find anything exciting?"

"Not really. It looks like we might have found an old mine shaft," Jerry said.

"Really? What would anybody be mining for around here?

Joseph spoke up. "A hundred years ago, some folks thought there might be gold or silver in these hills. I've found a number of test mines over the years. Usually they don't go but a few feet into the hill. Apparently they'd dig a little and give up when nothing turned up. I've found some antique shovels and picks in these sites. They actually bring a nice little price from collectors."

"You guys have done a lot of digging. Is it really worth it?"

"That's the problem," Joseph said. "You never know. Sometimes it is, sometimes it's not. So far today, it's not."

Jerry was surprised at the story Joseph had just told, and he couldn't tell if had satisfied Werner. He was a little suspicious. Would this guy walk a half-mile into the woods just to see how they were doing? He wondered if Werner suspected they were up to something more than what they said.

"You must have found this yesterday. You don't have your metal detectors with you," Werner said.

"We left the equipment in the truck. Those batteries go quickly, so I won't even get them out until we absolutely need it." Joseph said.

Jerry decided it was time to try and change the subject. "So Craig, how long have you been with the Resort?"

"Almost ten years. Since the beginning. I know this property like the back of my hand."

The perfect opening Jerry thought. "It doesn't look like we're having any luck here. Do you have anything to suggest? Where else on the property should we look?"

"I have no idea. Mr. Benton is the expert on metal detecting, not me."

Trying to put an end to the conversation, Joseph thanked Werner for checking on them. "Give our best to Maureen."

"Will do, and good luck. Seems like a lot of work for little or nothing."

"That's the thing with metal detecting. You never know," Joseph said.

As Werner was walking away, Jerry expressed his concern. "Do you think he knows anything?"

"How could he?"

"I have no idea. I don't trust him. Either he knows something, or he just asks too many questions. I don't like it . . . or him."

"Stop being a cop. He's just being friendly. I think he was a little embarrassed about yesterday and was trying to make up for it."

"I'm a trooper, not a cop, and I hope you're right."

They went back to their digging. As the work progressed, an entrance to a cave was coming into view. The excitement reached a climax when, near the top of the entrance, there seemed to be an opening. Some rocks were beginning to fall back into the opening. They tried to look inside but it was too dark to see anything. "Do you have a flashlight in your truck?" Joseph asked.

"Of course."

"Let's break for lunch." They had brought a cooler with sandwiches, soda and ice. Sitting on the open tailgate of the truck, Joseph told Jerry how he thought King Joseph was looking over them.

"That's creepy."

"This is it Jerry. I feel it in my bones. Don't you feel it?"

"I don't know. There is something there but I'm not sure it's your treasure."

"Why else would there be a manmade cave there."

"Maybe what you told Werner about a test mine was closer to the truth. How many of those test mines have you found in the past?"

"None."

"You're kidding. You just made that up?"

"Yup."

"We need to get back there and finish this. We're almost there."

"Where's your flashlight?"

"It's on the floor behind the driver's seat."

Joseph went to the cab and got the flashlight and the two walked back to the site.

Looking up at the opening in the mound, Jerry could see Joseph was hesitating. He knew his friend was trying hard not to get too excited. "Go ahead," he said. "It's your treasure."

Joseph climbed to the opening and looked in with the flashlight. As he looked inside, tears started forming in his eyes. He wiped them away.

Jerry knew what was happening. "You did it, didn't you?"

There was no response, just a head nod. Joseph hoped his eyes weren't playing tricks, that it wasn't a dream. He wiped more tears away.

Thirty years of wondering, hoping, researching and keeping secrets had come to an end. He sat up and still didn't say a word. He motioned to Jerry to take the flashlight and have a look. Jerry climbed the mound and took the light from Joseph.

Looking inside, he saw more than fifty wooden boxes stacked into piles of three and four. One box was different than the rest. It was a little smaller, with darker wood and elegantly carved. Jerry couldn't tell what the carving was.

He backed away and looked over to see Joseph sitting on a rock with his head in his hands. "You found it buddy. Congratulations. Come on, we need to get in there and get this to the truck. Are you Okay?"

Joseph looked up and took one final wipe of his eyes. "I'm fine, just a little emotional. All these years. Thank you, Jerry, for everything you have done for me. You've been a good friend."

"Stop blubbering and get to work. We have a lot to do."

Joseph got up, "Yeah, we do have a lot to do. You gonna just stand there or what?"

It was another hour of moving rocks and dirt away from the entrance of the cave before they could comfortably get inside. The entire space was four feet wide, ten feet deep and six feet high. Joseph went directly to a stack of four boxes with the darker wooden box on top. There were carvings on all four sides. "Spanish oak," Joseph said. "Look at this." He pointed the flashlight to the top of the box where a single image had been carved. Joseph knew exactly what it was.

"That, my bald-headed friend, is the Coat of Arms of Joseph Bonaparte, King of Spain. If my hunch is right, this box holds the royal crown."

Joseph reached for the box. It was heavier than he'd expected. For a moment he let his fingers caress the carving on the top of the box. The latch was rusty, but he was able to open it. The inside of the top of the box was lined with an aged, heavy, dark red velvet cloth. Another piece of heavy velvet covered the contents. He carefully pulled back the fabric to reveal the crown. There was a thick band of gold at the base. The band was encrusted with bright red rubies and brilliant blue sapphires ranging in size from a quarter inch to a full inch in diameter. There was a red velvet cap attached to the inside of the band. Seven arches of gold, inlaid with diamonds, curved over the cap from the gold band to a gold ball above the center. On top of the ball was a golden cross.

Jerry just stared. "Unbelievable."

Joseph didn't take the crown out of the box. Without saying a word, he looked at Jerry with a smile and gently closed the lid. He motioned to the other boxes. "Let's see what's in these."

Jerry took a large knife from his belt and pried open another box. The wood was soft pine and beginning to rot. He pulled back the wool fabric that covered the contents. Six gold bars appeared. They sat on another layer of fabric that covered six larger silver bars. Worried the box would fall apart, he tried to lift it. It held.

"We need to get this out of here." They spent another hour moving rocks to make it easier to remove their find. Jerry positioned the wheelbarrow at the bottom of the rock pile. Each box weighed forty to fifty pounds. Only four boxes would fit in the wheelbarrow at a time. Joseph manned the wheelbarrow on the first trip to the truck. He handed Jerry the oak box with the crown, "Can you carry this?"

"It would be a pleasure."

A light rain was beginning to fall, and it was a struggle maneuvering the wheelbarrow through the woods. The four pine boxes were loaded in the bed of the truck. The crown was carefully placed on the floor of the cab. It was almost six hours before the entire contents of the cave were loaded. And they weren't all easy trips. The bottoms of several boxes had rotted completely and the contents had to be stacked separately. While Jerry covered the boxes with the tarp, Joseph returned to the site to collect the tools and take one last look at the now empty cave.

He couldn't help but think how difficult it must have been 180 years ago to cover the opening of the cave and leave the treasure behind. "I'm not sure I could have done that," he said softly.

Silently, he looked up and thanked Joseph Bonaparte.

FORTY-TWO

DURING THE drive back to Cranberry Lake, Jerry asked Joseph if he found the written permission he had received from the Resort.

"I did, but it took a while. I was beginning to panic a little last night. It wasn't in the file with the resort documents. Apparently, when your buddies at the state police were going through the files they collected during their search, they put it back in the wrong folder. It took me two hours to find it."

"Do you know what could have happened if you didn't have it?"

"Yea, bad stuff."

"If you didn't have that letter, I would have had to confiscate the treasure and turn it over to the state police. It would have become the property of the Resort."

Joseph opened the glove box and found the envelope with several white pages folded inside. He had put it there right after Jerry picked him up that morning. The papers included the letter of permission as well as the provisions of New York State law regarding lost and found property.

"My lawyer gave me a copy of these when he drew up the letter of permission for the Resort. He drafted the letter for me when I made the investment. He says the letter is rock solid and it gives me ownership of anything I find."

"Good. I need a copy of that too," Jerry said. "To protect us both. If the letter clearly states you have ownership of anything you find, then we don't ever have to report it."

"I'll make you copies of everything as soon as we get home."

As they approached Joseph's driveway he turned to Jerry, "I have one more secret I've been keeping from you."

"Really, what's that?"

"Let's get this stuff inside and you'll see."

They carried the treasure to the bedroom and stacked the boxes and loose bars near the end of the bed. "Is this going to be safe here?" Jerry wondered.

"Very safe." Joseph turned to the south wall where there was an oversized wardrobe. In all the years they had been friends, Jerry had only been in the bedroom a few times and never really noticed this large piece of furniture. It had to be seven feet tall. There were double doors with brass handles. It looked Early American in style, but Jerry wasn't sure. Unlike most wardrobes, this had a heavy lock built into the doors. It was very well built. Overbuilt, he thought.

Joseph pulled the keys from his pocket and opened the doors. The inside was stuffed with hanging clothes. Joseph grabbed several hangers and placed them on the bed.

"That lock is a bit of overkill to protect some clothes, don't you think?" Looking at the clothes, Jerry asked, "Are these all new?"

"Not really, but I've never worn any of them," he said. They're just for show."

"What do you mean, for show? Nobody will ever see them if they stay locked inside a wardrobe."

"Just wait." Once all the clothes were removed, Jerry reached inside. A quick pull on a hidden latch, and the entire back panel opened into the wardrobe itself. A light automatically turned on revealing a six foot by eight foot hidden room.

Jerry stood there, staring in amazement.

The light came from a single bulb in the ceiling. The bare walls were pine slats. It looked like the interior of a large cedar closet, without the cedar.

Joseph knocked on the wood slats, "Steel reinforced poured concrete behind this."

Jerry sat on the edge of the bed and shook his head. "You really are a man of mystery."

"I built this because I hoped someday I would need it. I always believed this day would come."

"You're remarkable."

Jerry's arm was aching from the day's activity, but Joseph was happy to pack the treasure in the vault by himself. When he finished, he left the clothes on the bed, and closed and locked the wardrobe doors.

"Let me buy you dinner."

"You're on."

They took their usual table at the lodge. Ashley was off, and Caitlin was their waitress. Both ordered diet cola.

"So, you're now a rich man. There has to be several hundred million dollars there. What do you do now?"

"I'm not sure. I've always dreamed of finding the treasure, but I never actually thought of what I would do when I did find it. My dreams never went this far. First, I've got to do an inventory and figure out how much is there. After that, I don't know. One thing I do know, I want to return the crown to Joseph."

"What do you mean?"

"Joseph is buried in a very famous museum in Paris. It's called *Les Invalides*."

"I've heard of it."

"It's where Napoleon himself is buried. It was originally built as a hospital and retirement home for French war veterans. Now, it's a whole complex of buildings with museums and monuments all relating to French military history. I saw it when I went to Paris several years ago."

"You told me about that."

"I want Joseph to have his crown back."

"You know, the Spanish government will bitch like hell. They'll want it themselves."

"Maybe," Joseph said. "I'll let the French and Spanish fight that out. I'll feel better if I give it to Joseph. But if it ends up back in Spain, I won't be too upset. Jerry, I want you to go with me when I return it. We'll let King Joseph pay for our trip. I don't think he'll mind, and I think there's enough there to cover our expenses."

"I've never been to Paris. I'd love to go. Do you have any idea what you'll do after that?"

"If I tell you, you'll think I'm crazy."

"I already think you're crazy."

"I've done a lot of research over the years. Not just this, but about the Adirondacks and legends of other lost treasures. One's not too far from where we were today.

"You've got to be kidding me. You're not serious."

"I am serious. There's this guy named Moses Follensby. He was an English army officer, supposedly of noble birth."

"Any connection to Follensby Pond?"

"The same. It's just a few miles southeast of Tupper Lake. Anyway, legend has it he buried $400,000 near his cabin. Do you have any idea what that would be worth today? And there's another one. It's on an island in the St. Lawrence River near Ogdensburg. The story goes that in the mid-1700s a French commander buried two hundred pounds of gold before surrendering his fort to the British."

Jerry couldn't believe what he was hearing. "You planning on becoming a professional treasure hunter?"

"Maybe. I was thinking. You're close to retirement. Your share of what we found today means you'll never have to work again. To hell with your pension. I thought maybe we could go into business together. We could call it J & J Investments."

Jerry sipped on his diet cola and thought for a minute. "That's an interesting proposition. I have just one question."

"What's that?"

"Whose 'J' comes first?"

AUTHOR'S NOTE

WHEN WRITING a novel with so many historical facts, I thought it appropriate to take the time to separate fact from fiction for the reader.

First, and most important, *all* the characters in this book are fictional, with the exception of the historical figures and Christopher Westbrook, director of The Ranger School in Wanakena, New York. Regarding the others, every author does use characteristics and traits from people in their real lives to develop their fictional characters.

The historical foundation in the prologue is true. Events regarding Napoleon and his brother Joseph, while in Naples, Sicily, Spain and France, all happened as described. Joseph Bonaparte was born in Corte, the capital of the Corsican Republic. The year after his birth, Corsica was conquered by France. His given name was Giuseppe Bonaparte.

Everything regarding James D. Le Ray and his vast property holdings in upstate New York is also true. In fact, there is a town in Jefferson County, New York, named Le Ray and three towns were named after his children, Alexander (Alexandria Bay), Vincent (Cape Vincent) and Theresa.

The meeting in 1815 that took place between Le Ray and Joseph Bonaparte in Blois, France, after Joseph fled Spain, actually happened as described, including the wagons full of silver. This is where Le Ray agreed to sell Joseph Bonaparte the one hundred fifty thousand acres of land with the lake. There are versions of the story in which Joseph purchased less than thirty thousand acres, but the more reliable sources tend toward one hundred fifty thousand acres.

Benjamin Franklin did live at the estate of Le Ray's father during his stay in France.

The final decision to write this book occurred when I read newspaper accounts of the fire at the Bonaparte home in Bordentown, New Jersey. These accounts talked about secret panels that led to rooms where the royal crown and other treasures were stored, and ultimately rescued. The accounts also mentioned how the contents of the wine vaults were saved that night by being rolled down a secret seventy-foot tunnel to the river. These newspaper accounts never mentioned what the contents of the wine vaults actually were, although the reports did describe how associates of Bonaparte were severely burned while saving these items. For purposes of this novel, I preferred to believe that nobody would risk their life to save a little wine. Rather, I believe the casks retrieved from the wine vaults that night contained the Spanish Royal Treasure.

Fact or fiction? You decide.

Local newspaper accounts in upstate New York do tell of the former King arriving at Lake Bonaparte with a large entourage and, "with carriages drawn by six horses each." I always wondered why so many horses were needed, unless of course, the carriages and wagons were loaded down with vast amounts of silver, gold and jewels. Again, this is simply my conjecture. I'll let you decide.

Finally, while he lived in America, Joseph Bonaparte did have an illegitimate daughter, Caroline, with an American mistress. Caroline married Col. Zebulon Benton of Jefferson County, New York. The Benton family was originally from Ogdensburg. France ultimately recognized Caroline as a legitimate princess. Col. Zebulon Benton and Princess Caroline Bonaparte Benton are buried near the old Presbyterian Church in Oxbow,

New York. Their graves can still be seen today.

Joseph Benton is completely fictional.

The Dumas Cipher, mentioned in chapter three, is real, and was used extensively during the Revolutionary War to protect war plans from the British. It was also the primary cipher used by Benjamin Franklin while he was the American representative to the French court. Several alternative ciphers were suggested to Franklin, but he preferred the Dumas.

Of course, the French author Alexandre Dumas is real. His father was a general in Napoleon's army. Dumas is the author of numerous plays and books. The most famous being *The Count of Monte Cristo* and *The Three Musketeers*.

The shift of magnetic north, first mentioned in chapter eight, is factual. In Tupper Lake, the 7°14' difference between magnetic north in 1830 and today is also true. As described in the book, there are airports around the country, including Tampa International, which have had to change their runway numbers because of this magnetic shift.

Just like Joseph Benton in chapter eight, I actually did send an e-mail to the chairman of the geology department at Rensselaer Polytechnic Institute in Troy, New York, the oldest and one of the most respected engineering schools in America. I said I was an author, and needed help determining the shifts in magnetic north. I got a return e-mail, with answers, within forty-eight hours. By the way, the real chairman, Dr. Frank Spear, does specialize in metamorphic petrology. And, I still don't know what that is.

The same e-mail story is true regarding Christopher Westbrook, director of The Ranger School in Wanakena, New York, which offers their students a unique educational experience in a spectacular natural setting in the heart of the Adirondack Park. I can't imagine a more beautiful and practical place to study. The school is part of the State University of New York, College of Environmental Science and Forestry.

In chapter twenty-three, the brief story about Verplanck Colvin, surveyor and "father of the Adirondack Park," is true. The information in this chapter about the surveyors Lewis & Clark, Mason & Dixon, Thomas Jefferson and George Washington is also accurate.

Sun Tzu's, *The Art of War*, first mentioned in chapter two, is real. Written more than twenty-five hundred years ago, it is still one of the best business strategy books available today.

Of course, the New York State Police are real, as are their Bureau of Criminal Investigation and the Forensic Investigation Unit. The State Police forensics garages in Ray Brook and Olean, New York, are also real. The New York State Police Forensic Investigation Unit is reportedly one of the best forensics units in America.

We all owe a great debt of gratitude to the men and women of the State Police who risk their lives daily to protect us. If you happen to see a New York State Trooper, even if they are giving you a speeding ticket, thank them for their courage and dedication.

All of the geographic locations in the book are real, including Lake Bonaparte and the Bonaparte Cave State Forest.

In chapter one, the controversy over the size of Cranberry Lake is true. Even today, many websites and brochures list the shoreline as 155 or 165 miles. The actual shoreline is 55 miles.

At this writing, there is a major resort development being planned for the very real Big Tupper Ski area property. It is similar in size and scope to the fictional Adirondack Mountain and Lake Resort, but that's where the similarity ends.

Specific locations, like the Cranberry Lake Lodge and Stone Manor

Diner in Cranberry Lake, The Bookstore Plus in Lake Placid, T. F. Finnigan's Men's Shop in Saranac Lake, the Tail O' the Pup in Ray Brook and the Crowne Plaza Hotel & Restaurant in Lake Placid, are all real. And, they're all great places. Stop by and visit them on your trip to the Adirondacks . . . and say hi for me.

The Fairview Motel in Ray Brook, where Judge Kelly's vehicle is found in chapter ten, is fictional.

The Adirondack Park, of course, is real. It is the largest park in the lower 48 states. I have traveled much of the world and most of the United States, and I still think this park is the most beautiful place on this planet. And it's a wonderful place to live.

The geological information about the Adirondack Mountains and surrounding areas is also accurate. The "Forever Wild" motto for the Adirondacks *is* enshrined in the New York State Constitution.

The Adirondack Park Agency is real, but any similarity between their actions in this book and reality are completely coincidental. The real Adirondack Park Agency has a difficult job, balancing wise use of the land with economic development. The concept of balancing wise use with economic development is often easy to write about, but quite difficult to execute in the real world.

There are many fine environmental groups based in the Adirondacks. Adirondack Environmental Watch is completely the product of my imagination. It is not based on any group, past or present.

Tree spiking, mentioned in chapter two, has occurred in the northwestern regions of the United States, and radical environmentalists have been convicted. I am not aware of any tree spiking having ever taken place in the Adirondacks.

In chapter forty-two, the laws in New York State regarding "lost and found treasure," are real. Also in chapter forty-two, the information about the Paris museum, *Les Invalides*, is accurate.

Finally, there are stories of other lost treasures in the Adirondacks. In chapter forty-two, the Moses Follensby treasure and the treasure buried by a French Commander on an island in the St. Lawrence River have been rumored for years. Who knows, down the road you may find Joseph and Jerry looking for other lost treasures in the Adirondacks.

So, does the Adirondack Treasure really exist? Is the Spanish Royal Treasure buried somewhere in the Adirondacks? All I can say is, maybe. Certainly, the rumors have been around for 180 years. And, one can easily interpret the available evidence to suggest it is real. There is no evidence that Joseph took it with him when he returned to France in 1838.

If it exists, where is it buried?

That, I don't know. If I did, I wouldn't have written this book, I'd be lying on a beach in Bora Bora in the winter and, of course, after the black flies left, I'd be in Cranberry Lake for the summer.

While evidence suggests that Joseph Bonaparte wasn't the brightest of men, I don't think even he would have buried the treasure on his own property. After all, King Ferdinand VII, whom Napoleon had deposed when he invaded Spain, and who then replaced Joseph after he fled Spain, was aware of Joseph's property on Lake Bonaparte. In fact, he allegedly sent a team of assassins to kill Joseph and recover the treasure.

Many people do believe it's at the bottom of Lake Bonaparte.

There is absolutely no evidence to suggest it is buried on the property of the Big Tupper Ski area. That was simply a convenient location to allow me to create the "developer verses environmentalist" part of the storyline.

If the treasure really exists, it is probably lost to history.

On the other hand . . . if you find it, call or send me an e-mail at

AdirondackTreasure@gmail.com.

Here is a little warning. If you're planning on searching for the treasure, the laws in New York State regarding the use of metal detectors are very strict, particularly on state owned land. If you are on private land without written permission, and happen to find the treasure, it belongs to the property owner.

Happy hunting!

Adirondack Treasure—Isle Royale

Savannah Christian finds among her late father's belongings a cryptic letter about gold he allegedly discovered while working construction on the St. Lawrence Seaway. The treasure, he said, had been buried on an island in the St. Lawrence River during the French and Indian War. When he died, Jack Christian left behind the letter and his personal journal, which Savannah believes tells where the treasure is currently buried. She has read the journal dozens of times, but has been unable to find any information that might be a clue to the location of the gold. Having recently seen newspaper stories about Joseph Benton finding his famous ancestor's royal crown and returning it to France, Savannah has sought out Joseph Benton and his friend Jerry Doolin for help.

Their search begins a series of adventures that will change their lives forever. A developing romance between Joseph and Savannah is complicated by the return of the mysterious Sharon Benton, Joseph's ex-wife. Jerry not only questions Sharon's motives for returning, but as the search for the treasure becomes more challenging it leads him to question if the treasure is real or simply a cover story for Jack Christian's sudden, and possibly ill-gotten, wealth. Friendships are once again tested. Romance, conflict and personal intrigue are about to collide with world events.

The Middle East is in turmoil. Egypt, Libya, Tunisia, Yemen, and Syria have all dealt with uprisings. Osama Bin Laden is dead. Ayman al-Zawahri is appointed to run al-Qaeda and is out to avenge the death of Bin Laden. In North Korea, Kim Jong Il is dead. His son, Kim Jong Un is now the Supreme Leader looking to solidify his newfound position. Together, al-Qaeda and North Korea are planning an event to let the world know they are still very much a force to be reckoned with.

The freighter Ares is berthed at the port of Ogdensburg, and the freighter Athena is headed toward Boston. Both are part of the plot that, if successful, would be devastating to the United States. The special EMP weapon hidden aboard one of the freighters could send the United States back to the Dark Ages. If it's detonated, US infrastructure would be crippled. The entire electrical grid and virtually all communications would be destroyed. All food production and transportation would come to a halt. The United States would be paralyzed, not for days or weeks, but for years. The stakes are high. The country is in grave danger unless the terrorists are stopped. United States intelligence has been on high alert for months, but nothing actionable has been developed.

After several trips in search of the gold, Joseph, Savannah and Jerry become entangled in the terrorists' plot when Jerry recognizes something is terribly wrong with the freighter he sees berthed at the wharf in Ogdensburg. The remarkable events that take place result in tense moments, life-threatening encounters, and Joseph, Jerry and Savannah's visit to the White House.

To meet the authors and to follow development of the new book, "like" Adirondack Treasure on Facebook.